BUXOM BONUS

Sheila Monroe had come to Skye Fargo's hotel room to beg him to try to rescue her son, Bobby, from the band of Sioux that had stolen him. Only a lowlife would take advantage of a woman in that position, Skye thought, even if the woman was as superbly voluptuous as Sheila most clearly was in her low-cut blouse and clinging skirt.

Now, though, the bargaining was over.

"You've made up your mind then—and nothing will change it?" Sheila asked.

"Afraid not," Skye said.

"Good," said Sheila.

And in front of Fargo's widening eyes, Sheila pulled the drawstring at the scooped neck of her blouse. The neckline fell wide open to reveal her in all her magnificence.

"No bargains, no trading-off, no deals," she said. "Now I can do it just because I want to...."

Exciting Westerns by Jon Sharpe from SIGNET

THE TRAILSMAN 51

SIOUX
CAPTIVE

by

Jon Sharpe

A SIGNET BOOK

NEW AMERICAN LIBRARY

PUBLISHER'S NOTE

This novel is a work of fiction. Names, characters, places, and incidents either are the product of the author's imagination or are used fictitiously, and any resemblance to actual persons, living or dead, events, or locales is entirely coincidental.

The first chapter of this book previously appeared in *Blood Oath*, the fiftieth book in this series.

SIGNET TRADEMARK REG. U.S. PAT. OFF. AND FOREIGN COUNTRIES
REGISTERED TRADEMARK—MARCA REGISTRADA
HECHO EN CHICAGO, U.S.A.

SIGNET, SIGNET CLASSIC, MENTOR, PLUME, MERIDIAN AND NAL BOOKS
are published by New American Library,
1633 Broadway, New York, New York 10019

First Printing, March, 1986

1 2 3 4 5 6 7 8 9

PRINTED IN THE UNITED STATES OF AMERICA

The Trailsman

Beginnings . . . they bend the tree and they mark the man. Skye Fargo was born when he was eighteen. Terror was his midwife, vengeance his first cry. Killing spawned Skye Fargo, ruthless, cold-blooded murder. Out of the acrid smoke of gunpowder still hanging in the air, he rose, cried out a promise never forgotten.

The Trailsman, they began to call him, all across the West: searcher, scout, hunter, the man who could see where others only looked, his skills for hire but not his soul, the man who lived each day to the fullest, yet trailed each tomorrow. Skye Fargo, the Trailsman, the seeker who could take the wildness of a land and the wanting of a woman and make them his own.

*1860, the wild land of western Montana
in the shadow of the Sapphire Mountains . . .*

1

"This was a nice morning until you came along, honey," the big man with the lake-blue eyes muttered.

"Abigail, I told you. Abigail Snow," the young woman snapped.

"A white-winged dove sang real pretty. This little stream made a nice tinkly sound, and the pocket gophers set up a soft chatter," the big man went on. "Since you showed up I've heard nothing but your cackling."

"That's just too damn bad," the young woman threw back, her lips tight. The big man surveyed her again as he bent down to the stream to fill his canteen. She had light brown hair cut short and full of curls, direct brown eyes, a thin nose, and a long, narrow figure with modest breasts that pushed upward against a light blue cotton blouse. She'd be really pretty if she stopped holding her face so prim and severe, he decided. "Hasn't the thought of being a good Samaritan ever crossed your mind, Mr. Fargo?" she snapped.

"Yes, ma'am, and it usually crosses right on out," Skye Fargo answered as he finished filling the canteen.

"I've offered you good money," she said.

"And I answered you on that," he returned.

He watched her mouth thin as he rose to his feet and tightened the lid on the canteen.

"Dammit, a Sioux runs off with a helpless little boy. Doesn't that reach you at all? Don't you feel anything?" she accused.

"I feel sorry," he said.

"Is that all? Have you no conscience?"

"I've a conscience. I let common sense keep it down," he answered.

"Meaning what?" She glared.

"Meaning that that Sioux could be anywhere by now and the boy dead. It happened a week ago, you say," Fargo told her.

"But maybe he's still alive. We have to try to find him," the young woman insisted.

"It's plain he's not your boy." Fargo frowned at her.

"He's my sister's boy," Abigail said.

He shrugged. "Makes no matter. I told you, I've got a job to do," he said.

"I knew that before you told me," she said, and he lifted one thick black eyebrow. "You're going to Ironwood to pick up a wagon train. That's why I chased after you. My sister lives just outside town."

"Who told you all this, honey?" Fargo asked.

"Ben Hibbs," she said, and Fargo half smiled. Ben was a post rider who knew pretty much what everyone was up to in his territory. He let his gaze move out from the little glen by the stream. Low hills surrounded it on three sides, a perfect spot to rest and relax. Or it had been, he grunted as Abigail's voice cut into his thoughts, an edge of accusation in it. "You could combine both jobs," she pushed at him.

He tossed her a glance of pained tolerance. "Can't break trail for a wagon train and go chasing some crazy Sioux," Fargo said.

"You could give it a try," she said, and suddenly a note of desperate pleading had come into her voice. He eyed her narrow, high-busted figure and saw her try to keep the pleading out of her face as she continued to regard him accusingly.

"I'd do right by no one," Fargo answered, and a tiny frown touched his brow. "Why'd you come looking for me? Why not the boy's mother?" he asked.

"There are reasons. They don't concern you unless you're taking the job," she said stiffly.

"Fair enough," he agreed. "Sorry, go find yourself another tracker."

"I can't. It'd take too long," she snapped angrily. "Besides, I'm told you're the very best."

"And I told you I'm spoken for. I've given my word. I won't go back on it," he said as he hung the canteen on the saddle and stroked the magnificent black-and-white Ovaro.

"Your word to a bunch of farmers and misfits looking for a new start. They can wait." She sniffed disdainfully.

"You see things as it suits you to see them." He smiled. "But then, that's what most folks do. But I made an agreement. I'll stand by it."

Anger flared in the direct brown eyes, and her

pretty face grew hard. "Or maybe it's just a lot safer to lead a wagon train than to track down a Sioux," she speared waspishly.

She was calling him a coward, but he laughed as he refused to take the bait. "Might be," he agreed pleasantly.

"Damn you," she swore as she spun on her heel and strode back to her horse. He watched her halt alongside the animal and rest her forehead against the saddle skirt for a moment. When she raised her head, she turned again and walked back to where Fargo waited beside the little stream. Her face now held resignation in it, and there was a sad beauty to her. "Maybe you'll think about it some more," she said. "I'm asking that of you."

"Fair enough," he said, and she thrust a piece of paper at him.

"That's where you can reach me in Ironwood in case you change your mind," she said.

Under the demanding anger her concern for the boy was plainly very real, he realized. He felt sorry for her, but he wouldn't go back on his word. But he had no wish to pull all hope out from under her, and he took the piece of paper and pushed it into his pocket. He returned to his horse with her, halted there as she started to move on. He spied that one of the saddle strings had come loose and had bent down to fix it when the shot exploded in the little glen. He felt the bullet graze the side of his head, and he pitched forward onto the ground as the horse instinctively skittered away. Abigail's scream cut through the air as he lay facedown and motionless.

The shot had come from the low rise to the north, the gunman undoubtedly still in position to fire again. It was time to play possum or he'd draw another shot that wouldn't miss. He lay still and listened to the sound of a horse galloping closer, skidding to a halt, and the rider slide from the saddle.

"Get the hell back, sister," he heard the man's voice rasp.

Fargo's eyes seemed to be closed but tiny, unnoticeable slits gave him a narrow view of nearby objects. He heard the footsteps walk toward him and halt. He felt the toe of the man's boot wedge itself under his chest. The man pushed and lifted with his foot, and Fargo let himself be turned limply onto his back. Through his slitted eyelids he glimpsed the end of the man's rifle barrel. He'd have but one chance, he knew, as the man's legs came into his view, but he continued to play dead.

He felt the man kick him in the side, and he let his body shake lifelessly. The man was plainly uncertain, and Fargo saw the rifle barrel lower as the man bent over him for a closer check. Fargo tensed his muscles, held still a fraction longer, and suddenly flung his right arm stiffly outward to slam into the man's ankles with the force of a two-by-four.

"Shit," the man cursed as he toppled forward, the rifle firing as his finger tightened on the trigger. Fargo felt the shot plow into the ground alongside him, but he was rolling now as the gunman pitched forward, half over him. He got one knee up and sank it into the man's ribs as the bushwhacker fell across him. He heard the man grunt in pain. Fargo continued to roll, halted his momentum, and came up on one knee to see the man, the rifle still in his hands, fire from half on his side.

Fargo flung himself sideways onto the ground as the rifle blast passed over his head. He rolled again and dived into a thicket of heavy underbrush. He yanked the big Colt from its holster as the bushwhacker fired again. Fargo heard the bullet snapping off twigs and leaves as it passed through. But he had the Colt aimed as the man realized that he was out in the open and tried to scramble for the brush behind him. Fargo fired, and the man cried out in pain as he clutched at his leg and fell. But he still clung to his rifle, and Fargo saw him try to pull the gun around to fire. The Colt barked again, and the rifle flew into the air as the man cursed and clutched at his right hand. He started to scramble for the bushes again when Fargo's shot threw up a little geyser of soil directly in front of his face. The man froze in place, one bleeding hand still dug into the ground. Fargo's quick glance saw that Abigail had backed to one side, her eyes round and wide with fright. He returned his gaze to the man still in place on the ground.

"You stay right there, you bushwhacking son of a bitch," Fargo said. "I want some answers out of you."

"Go to hell," the man snapped as he half turned onto his back.

Fargo let the click of the hammer being drawn back on the Colt sound through the little glen. "Talk or I'm going to shoot you apart piece by piece," he growled.

"Screw you, mister," the man returned. Fargo let the Colt fire, and a toe of the man's left foot blew away. The man screamed in pain and drew his leg up as he stared down at his bloodied foot.

"Talk," Fargo growled from the brush.

14

"Goddamn bastard," the man shouted back, pain in his voice. Fargo fired again, and this time the man's right kneecap erupted in a shower of blood and bone chips. The man cried out as he rolled onto his side in pain. "Goddamn," he said breathlessly, and clutched at his leg.

"Piece by piece," Fargo repeated from the thicket.

"You son of a bitch," the man cursed.

Fargo fired again and this time the man's right elbow disintegrated, and he half flew onto his other side as his wild scream of pain echoed. "Piece by piece," Fargo said again.

"All right, shit . . . all right," the man shouted in pain and terror. "I'll talk, I'll talk."

Fargo half rose in the thicket, his gun still aimed at the man. Abigail had remained in place, and she stared at the man on the ground with a frown. "I'm waiting," Fargo said. "And I'm out of patience."

Fargo saw the man, curled up in pain, start to lick his lips as the rifle shot exploded. Fargo dropped down, an instant, automatic reaction. But even as he did so he saw the figure on the ground grab at his chest as the shot slammed into him. Fargo's eyes flashed to the nearest hilltop in time to see the horse's gray rump disappear down the other side of the rise.

"Goddamn," he swore as he stood up and stepped out of the thicket. The man on the ground was rapidly becoming a huge, lifeless red stain that spread from his shattered chest. Fargo shot a glance at Abigail. "You all right?" he asked, and she nodded, shock still in her face.

His eyes returned to the low rise, and he cursed softly. By the time he mounted the Ovaro, the bushwhacker would be at the bottom of the rise and racing hard into thick tree cover. He brought his gaze back to the crumpled object that lay at his feet and grimaced. "Shit," he muttered again as he stared down at the lifeless form, and Abigail slowly moved to stand beside him.

"What'd you expect he'd tell you?" Abigail asked. "It's plain they were a pair of saddle bums who thought they'd found an easy dollar."

"Were they?" Fargo said as he turned his lake-blue eyes on her.

"Of course." Abigail frowned back.

"Try again," Fargo answered.

Her frown deepened. "What are you saying?" she asked.

"I'm saying that they were no bushwhackers out for an easy dollar. They were here to make sure you didn't hire me," he told her, and watched her lovely lips fall open.

"That's impossible. It's crazy," Abigail protested.

"Why'd they only try to nail me?" Fargo pushed at her.

"I guess they figured with you out of the way they could have their way with me," she returned.

"Good enough, except it doesn't fit these two. They were watching from the low rise but didn't make a move until they saw you give me that piece of paper," he said.

"Meaning what?" Abigail asked.

"From where they were it looked as though you'd given me the money to seal the deal, and I'd taken it. That's when the first one fired," Fargo said. Abigail's frown held as her brown eyes grew darker. "When the attack backfired, an ordinary bushwhacker would have taken off. But the second one waited until he heard the other one say he'd talk. He made sure he didn't and then hightailed it."

Abigail's face held protest and shock, mingled with disbelief. "Why?" she murmured. "Why would anyone want to stop me from trying to save a little boy's life?"

Fargo shrugged, his handsome, intense face made of chiseled stone. "I thought maybe you'd tell me," he said.

2

"I can't tell you anything because there's nothing to tell," Abigail Snow said. "What you're saying makes no sense at all. It's ridiculous."

"Maybe, but it's also true," Fargo maintained quietly.

Her short curly hair danced vigorously as she shook her head. "No, it can't be. You're reading it all wrong. You're jumping to conclusions," she insisted.

"Whatever you say, honey," he answered, and turned to the Ovaro.

"Don't patronize me," she flared. He shrugged and put one foot in the stirrup. "What about him?" she asked, nodding to the figure on the ground. "Aren't you going to bury him, at least?"

Fargo met her eyes with an icy stare. "You think he'd be doing that for me if he'd nailed me with that first shot?" he asked.

"Probably not," she admitted. "But two wrongs don't make a right," she added reprovingly.

"Maybe not, but they don't make me feel obligated, either," Fargo muttered as he swung onto the pinto.

"You're a stubborn man, Fargo." Abigail frowned. "And you still think you're right about those two bushwhackers."

"Go to the head of the class," he grunted as the Ovaro moved forward.

"You're not right. It just can't be," Abigail flung back. "It just doesn't make any sense." The direct brown eyes were filled with more than protest, he saw. The thought was obviously too shattering for her to accept. He found it pretty damn hard to understand, too, he admitted silently. The whole thing was growing more and more distasteful, and he wanted no part of it. Abigail came up alongside him on her brown mare. Her face was held stiff, as though she could hold pain outside herself. For all her prim strictness she somehow seemed like a little girl trying to play grown-up, her narrow figure and modest breasts adding to a young-filly quality about her. But refusing to face truth would only hurt her more in the long run, and he drew a deep sigh from inside himself.

"You going back to Ironwood?" he asked, and she nodded. "I'll ride along with you. It's not safe for a young woman to be riding out here alone," he told her.

"Thank you," she said, a faint note of surprise in her voice. "I appreciate that. It shows you're not entirely without conscience."

"Don't let it go to your head," he grunted, and put the Ovaro into a trot. He took a path northwest through two low hills of heavy green timber, mostly aspen and alders, and Abigail stayed beside him.

She rode well, he noted, her body moving easily with the horse, breasts swaying in unison. Her real prettiness returned as she relaxed some. "What are you doing out here in the Montana territory?" he asked.

"I came out to visit my sister six months ago. George Grizzard, he owns the bank in Ironwood, found out that I used to do bookkeeping back in Kansas and hired me to stay on to help him," Abigail explained.

"You going to set down out here for good?" Fargo asked.

"I doubt it," Abigail said. "This country frightens me. It's too wild, too untamed, too much of everything. It's not just the Indians. It's all just so terribly overpowering. It makes me feel helpless."

"I can see where that'd bother you." Fargo chuckled. "You like to be in control of the things around you."

"People with a backward sense of priorities bother me, too," she snapped in return, and he laughed again as his eyes swept the lush hill country, the towering mountain peaks just ahead, the thick, lush greenery and crags that were northwest Montana. It was indeed an untamed place, this land that formed the northern tip of the Rockies. The Spaniards had given it its name, *Montana*, place of mountains, and they'd been accurate enough, though there was plenty of high plains country amid the high hills. Though the Sioux roamed far and wide across the territory, the Northern Cheyenne, Crow, Kootanei and Assiniboin guarded their own areas with fierce pride. It was not a land for the amateur, and yet they came, many of them prospectors lured by the gold and silver imbedded in the rugged hills, others following the promise of rich, fertile land that lay ready for the taking. But they quickly found that there was a price, a price paid in lives and heartbreak that was too high for too many.

He halted on a ridge and let his gaze move slowly across the land. Watching for signs of Indians was automatic, but his eyes swept the land behind him and traveled in a half circle along the paths they had just ridden. Autumn was just starting to touch the land, the thick green expanse interrupted with a flash of scarlet here, a burst of yellow there, brilliant harbingers of the colorful tapestry that was yet to come. He moved on, Abigail beside him, and rested the horses twice more before the day began to slip into dusk. Each time he scanned the land behind as well as the rolling hills that lay ahead.

Resting beside a mountain stream, Abigail stretched herself out on the grass, half turned, and lifted her arms over her head. He watched the modest breasts pull upward and push against the cotton blouse. Once again he noted her sweet, young-girl loveliness. She caught him watching her, sat up, and drew primness into her face at once. He laughed. "You're afraid of a lot more than Indians and mountains, honey," he said.

"Such as?" she tossed back.

"You're afraid of yourself," he said.

"I'm not afraid to help a little boy in trouble," she flung back, and flounced to her feet.

"One for your side." He grinned and pulled himself onto the Ovaro. "Let's make time. It'll be dark soon."

She followed as he quickened the pace up through the hills. As he rode his eyes never stopped sweeping the terrain behind them and on both sides, and his lake-blue eyes had hardened as the sun disappeared behind the distant peaks of the Sapphire Mountain range. He pulled up in a thicket of alders with a small, half circle clearing in the center. The dusk deepened quickly, and the warmth of the day immediately gave way to a sharp night wind. "I'll make a small fire," Abigail said as she tethered the brown mare.

"No fire," he said sharply, and felt her eyes peering at him.

"You saw signs of something, didn't you? Indians, wasn't it?" she asked with alarm instant in her voice.

"Just taking no chances," he said placatingly, but suspicion stayed in her eyes as she took things out of her saddle bag. She had her own strips of beef jerky, and he sat near her to eat as the night closed down. A sliver of a new moon allowed only the faintest hint of pale light to penetrate the darkness, and he watched as Abigail finished eating, then started to go behind one of the trees to change. "Hell, you can undress right here for all I can see," Fargo remarked.

"I'm sure you can see a lot better than you'd tell me," she said as she disappeared behind the low branches. He smiled to himself. She hadn't been entirely wrong; his wild-creature's eyesight was remarkably good in the night. He had learned long ago not to strain his eyes peering through the dark but to let the night come to him, taking on its shapes and shadows to form its own dark patterns. He rose, set out his own bedroll, took off only his jacket and shirt, and was inside the bedroll when

Abigail returned, all but lost inside a big wool bath-robe.

He watched her crawl under her blanket and lay still, then sat up and placed his hat at the edge of his bedroll. He slid deep down inside the bedroll again, turned on his side, and drew his legs up. Slowly and silently he drew the big Colt from its holster, planted his elbow firmly against the ground, and leveled the gun at the half circle of trees across the tiny clearing, his finger poised against the trigger. "Good night," he heard Abigail call softly, an edge of crossness in her voice.

"Sleep. We'll be getting an early start come morning," he said, and heard her turn on her side. He settled down, the Colt poised, and began to wait as the cougar waits, that combination of tension and calm that kept every muscle poised yet avoided fatigue. As every hunter of the wild realized by instinct, waiting was but another form of action. He had seen the signs ever since he had set off with Abigail. They had been there, just as he'd expected, easy enough to pick up, and now all he had to do was wait. Without the glow even a small fire would have sent out, the intruder would have to come in close.

Abigail had fallen asleep quickly, the even sound of her breathing drifting through the dark stillness. Fargo stayed motionless as time seemed to stand still. Suddenly he heard the sound he was waiting for, the faint rustle as branches were pushed aside. He let his ears see for him as he took in the sounds. Two sets of leaves being brushed back, the first shorter, quicker, the second a longer, sliding sound. The visitor had dismounted and pushed through the trees and brush on foot, his horse following along behind. The sounds suddenly ceased, and Fargo's eyes were fixed on the half circle of alders across from his bedroll.

He watched the dark shape materialize in the faint glimmer of moonlight and move toward the two bedrolls. Fargo's finger rested against the trigger of the Colt as the figure paused, spotted his hat, and started toward him. He lowered the Colt a fraction of an inch inside the bedroll—he wanted the shot to hit low, a thigh or a calf. He caught the dull glint of the gun in the man's hand. He waited until the figure halted only a half dozen feet from the end of his bedroll. "Hold it right there," Fargo growled, his voice muffled, yet clear enough for the man to hear. The figure stiffened, and Fargo saw the man's arm begin to come up with the gun. He fired the Colt just as the man went into a half crouch, and he cursed as the shot tore through the end of the bedroll to slam into the man's groin. Fargo sat up, pushed out of the bedroll as the half crouched figure flew backward, all but doubled in two, and he saw Abigail sit up with a half-gasped little cry.

He watched the man's bent-in-two form lay on the ground, both hands clutched to his groin, his legs drawn up in a fetal position. Fargo took a step toward the figure, saw one leg stretch out, and then the man shudder and lay still. "Shit," he muttered.

"What happened? What is it?" he heard Abigail ask as she got to her feet.

"Company," Fargo grunted. "Now you can make that fire." He saw her frown at him as he looked back at her. "Go on, get it started," he ordered, and bent over the man as Abigail began to gather small branches from the ground. Fargo rose, strode into the trees, and returned leading the gray horse as

24

Abigail got a small pyramid of twigs lit. She blew the flame into life, and the small glow spread across the half circle. Fargo felt her eyes watching him as he knelt down beside the lifeless figure.

"He's the one that got away," she murmured.

"Go to the head of the class," Fargo muttered as he finished going through the man's pockets, rose, and examined the contents of the saddlebag on the gray horse. "Nothing that says anything about him," he spat in disgust, and turned to Abbey. Her round, direct brown eyes were boring into him.

"He tried to sneak up on us," she said.

"To finish the job while I was asleep," Fargo said.

"Only you were awake, waiting for him," Abigail said, a frown furrowing her smooth brow. "Because you expected him. You knew he was coming."

"I figured he had to follow when he saw me ride off with you. He had to try again."

"You weren't concerned about my riding alone at all," Abigail said, her voice rising. "You were setting this up. You bastard," she bit out.

"Flattery will get you nowhere," Fargo said.

"You set it up, used me as part of the bait," Abigail muttered. "It was a mistake ever coming to find you. You're deceitful as well as callous."

"Tired too. I'm going to get some sleep now," he said.

"I can't sleep with . . . with *him* laying there," Abigail protested.

Fargo drew a sigh, walked to the figure on the ground, lifted the inert weight, and draped the man across the saddle. He led the horse out of the little thicket into the woods, administered a sharp slap

25

on its rump, and the gray trotted away to be quickly swallowed up in the night.

Abigail was beneath her blanket when he returned to the thicket and the little fire had burned itself into glowing embers. He undressed and slid into his bedroll, felt the little hole at the foot end of it with his toe. He stretched inside the bedroll as the cool night wind blew across his face. She lay awake, he knew, and he spoke softly from inside the bedroll.

"Still think they were just ordinary bushwhackers?" he asked. Her silence was loud in the stillness. He had expected as much. He heard her turn on her side finally, and he let sleep pull his eyes closed as the night wind softly swirled across the land.

The morning sun woke him with its warm caress. He pushed himself from his bedroll, caught the sound of running water, and walked a dozen yards through the alders to find a swift little stream, deep enough and wide enough to offer a place to bathe. He stripped down, washed dust and dirt from himself, and stretched out in a stream of warm sunlight that made its way through the trees.

He had just about dried off when he heard Abigail coming through the trees. She emerged by the stream, spotted him, and spun around to turn her back to him. "Would you please put some clothes on?" she called back severely.

"Why not?" he said affably. "Was just about to do that, anyway." He pulled on underwear and trousers, and Abigail turned, her eyes taking in the powerfully muscled torso, the clean, chiseled line of his body. She pulled her eyes away but not before they had lingered appreciatively.

"Can I trust you to wait below until I'm finished?" she said.

"This time," he said, and drew a sharp glance as he strode away to return to the thicket.

He led both horses to a bed of blue-stemmed wheat grass where they foraged hungrily. He had the Ovaro saddled by the time Abigail returned. Her face still glistened with a patina of water, and she rubbed her short, curly brown hair with a towel. She went behind an alder, dressed, and came out wearing a white blouse of stiff linen that all but masked the modest breasts. Yet she looked as pretty as a young filly, her body swaying gracefully as she walked to her horse. "Let's ride," Fargo said, and led the way out of the thicket. He found a stand of pears that provided a cool, refreshing breakfast as the sun quickly grew hot, and he moved the horses up a narrow pathway that leveled onto a gently rolling plain.

"We ought to make Ironwood before dark," he commented, and saw Abigail's lips tighten for an instant, but she said nothing until the sun passed through the noon sky.

"Anything that happened last night change your mind about helping me?" she asked cautiously.

"Nothing's changed keeping my word," he said, and watched her fall into angry silence. Thoughts that tumbled wildly inside her mirrored pain in her eyes. "Talking helps sometimes, especially if you're looking for answers," Fargo remarked.

"I wouldn't know where to start," she said, flinging words out in exasperated bursts. "It just can't be what you say. It's crazy, senseless."

He cast her a frowning glance. "You never

answered me. Why you?" he asked. "You're not the boy's mother."

"Sheila couldn't come. Sam wouldn't let her," Abigail said.

"Who's Sam?"

"Sam Monroe, my sister's husband," Abigail answered.

"The boy's father wouldn't let her try to get somebody to find the boy?" Fargo frowned in surprise.

"He's not Bobby's father. Bobby is Sheila's boy from her last marriage. Her husband was killed back in Kansas. Wagon turned over on him," Abigail explained.

"Are you saying Sam Monroe doesn't give a damn about the boy?" Fargo pressed.

Abigail paused in thought before she answered, her smooth brow furrowing. "I can't say that. He's always been good enough to the boy since Sheila married him two years ago, strict but good. But Sam Monroe says Bobby's dead for sure, and he won't let Sheila go chasing after something that's past changing."

"He's probably right," Fargo said soberly.

"And he could be wrong," Abigail snapped. "Sam Monroe's a strange, stubborn man. He's very hard to like—for me, at least. I think he won't let Sheila go after Bobby because he needs her at the store. He needs her to run part of his business, seeing as how he can hardly count."

"That's why you came to find me instead of your sister," Fargo said, and Abigail nodded. "But he wouldn't have any reason to stop you from trying to get someone to find Bobby." Fargo frowned.

"None. That's why none of this makes any sense," she said.

"Lots of things don't make sense until you've got all the pieces," Fargo commented. "Somebody didn't want you hiring me."

"Then there has to be some other reason, maybe something I wouldn't know about," Abigail said, and Fargo shrugged.

"You say Sam Monroe runs a store?" he queried.

"The town supply and trading store. He outfits anybody and anything, sells just about everything, and trades whatever can be traded. That's why he needs Sheila on the spot helping him. He lets her take care of all the record-keeping and counting," Abigail said. "But I'm not going to tell Sheila just to forget about Bobby. I'll find a way to go after him somehow." She spoke the last words accusingly and let them hang in the air. Fargo grimaced and was glad to see the wood buildings of Ironwood come into sight as the afternoon began to wind down. Abigail fell silent until they were almost at the town.

"I'll be riding on," she said then. "I gave you the address where you can find me. I'm staying with Sheila at the Monroe house. Will you be at the hotel?"

"A night or two, maybe. I'd welcome a regular bed for a change. I'd guess the folks waiting for me will want to pull out soon," he told her. The direct brown eyes held a final appeal in their stare. "I'm sorry." He half shrugged. "You're a good gal. Don't go getting yourself killed by foolishness."

"I'm sorry you're sorry," she snapped angrily, and cantered away, the short curly hair bouncing as she rode. He blew a sigh and watched her as she skirted the edge of the town, heading north. He turned the Ovaro and slowly rode into Ironwood, quickly taking the measure of the town as he went down the wide main street. The town had the natural advantage of nestling in the shadows of the Sapphire range at one end and good high plains country on both sides. Crowded, bustling, plenty of wagons and pack mules crowding the streets, Ironwood existed for people on their way to someplace else, a restless oasis in the middle of a wild and untamed land.

The dusk was quickly turning into darkness as Fargo spotted the two-story frame house that was the town hotel with its bed-and-board sign outside. Almost opposite the hotel he saw the dance-hall saloon, a weathered sign proclaiming it as DOLLY'S PLACE. The saloon was already noisy and busy. He rode on and drew to a halt at a loading platform outside a gray building where a lanky-figured man with a long, saturnine face eyed him from the edge of the platform. "I'm looking for the Anderson wagon train. Eight wagons, all Conestogas," Fargo said.

"Yep." The man nodded.

"You know where they've hauled up?" Fargo asked.

"They left," the man said, his gloomy face not changing expression.

"They *what*?" Fargo blurted out, his thick brows lifting.

"Left. Pulled out. Four days ago," the man said.

"No, can't be. They were waiting for me," Fargo said.

"Guess they decided not to wait 'cause they

pulled out, all eight of them. Saw them go myself," the man answered.

Fargo stared at the man as the wave of astonishment continued to swirl around him. "But they'd no reason to pull out without me. Hell, they hired me to ride trail for them, even paid me a binder to seal the agreement." He frowned. "I'm here a day early."

The lanky figure shrugged, his dolorous face unchanged. "Wouldn't know anything about that, mister, but they pulled out, every last one of them," he said. "Except the feller that was supposed to go along as a wheelwright. He's still around."

"Where can I find him?" Fargo asked quickly.

"He's been spending all his time at Dolly's Place, but I hear he's never sober enough to put a sentence together," the man said.

"He'll talk to me. You know his name?" Fargo growled.

"Ed Whiddle," the man said.

"Much obliged," Fargo said as he turned the Ovaro and trotted the horse back to the dance hall. He dropped the reins over the hitching post in the square of smoky yellow light that stretched out from the open doors of the saloon and stepped inside. Squinting through the smoke, he let his eyes grow accustomed to the light from an overhead chandelier. His gaze traveled across the long bar at the far end of the dance hall where a dozen men lined the chipped oak edge of the bar. None appeared especially drunk, and Fargo shifted his gaze to the bare, round tables that lined the big room. A half dozen girls were sprinkled among the customers there, and once again Fargo saw no one that fit the description he'd been given of Ed

Whiddle. He started to stroll across the room toward the bar when he saw the woman come across the floor toward him. She had a large, frowsy figure, even in her shiny blue dress, with too much paint and too many pounds.

"Hello, big stranger," she said as she halted in front of him. "What's your pleasure?"

"Looking for somebody, name of Ed Whiddle. Heard he spends a lot of time here," Fargo said.

The woman's fleshy face turned down. "Not anymore. I don't allow falling-down drunks in here, and that's what he is. He comes in, buys a bottle, and takes it outside someplace."

"I'll just wait for him," Fargo said.

"He's bought his first bottle already. He'll be back for another about midnight," she said, and her full face managed to produce a suggestive leer. "You could enjoy one of my girls till then. You'll have plenty of time. I'll call you when he shows," she said.

Fargo's eyes narrowed. Ironwood wasn't any St. Louis, but it was big enough for a drunk to find himself some hidden-away spot. Searching for Whiddle could be a painfully slow task. "Not tonight, honey," he answered the woman. "You know where Whiddle takes his bottle?"

Dolly's face fell sullenly. "I don't keep track of drunks," she snapped.

"It's worth the price of one of your girls," Fargo said, and saw a little glint come into the woman's eyes.

"I heard he holes up in the old lumberyard. That's out back of town," she said, and Fargo tossed her a silver dollar and turned away. "Come back for the right reasons next time, big boy," the madam called after him.

He went outside into the night and led the pinto down the dark streets by the cheek strap. A pale moon touched the darkened buildings of Ironwood, and he peered between the houses he passed. He'd almost reached the end of town when he spotted the old lumberyard behind the houses of the main street and guided the Ovaro toward it. The old place was not much more than a sagging shed with pieces of old planking scattered nearby. He picked his way along the splintered, broken pieces of planking, halted, and inclined his head as he listened. The sound came from the other side of the shed, a deep belch and a thick-tongued curse.

Fargo made his way around to the far side of the warped shed to see the man sitting on the ground, his back against the outer wall of the shed, a half emptied bottle of booze in his hand. Fargo stepped closer, halted in front of him. The man raised his head and peered up at the big figure that had appeared. Fargo saw Ed Whiddle try to focus bleary, reddened eyes, give up the task, and put the bottle to his lips. Fargo knelt down, and his lips drew back in distaste as he peered at the man. Ed Whiddle was stinking, stoned drunk. The man was in his late thirties, half balding, with a round face with soft, hanging jowls and a paunch bulging from his midsection. Fargo reached out, closed his hand on the man's shoulder, and shook him. "Can you hear me?" he asked.

Ed Whiddle started to topple sideways, and Fargo caught him, brought him back against the wall of the shed. "Lemme alone," Ed Whiddle muttered thickly. Fargo rose to his feet, thought about taking the bottle from the man, but discarded the thought. Another half dozen swigs of whiskey wouldn't make any difference now, and he wanted the man to stay in place. He turned, swung onto his horse, and rode back to the dance hall. The big woman saw him the minute he entered and came toward him at once.

"Didn't expect you back so soon, big man," she said.

"That makes two of us," Fargo growled. The madam's practiced eyes peered at him sharply.

"You come back for the wrong reasons again?" she said.

"You get the cigar, and I get a big pot of hot coffee," Fargo said, and she frowned at him.

"What the hell are you talking about, mister?" the woman said.

"You make coffee here. Every saloon does. I want a big pot of it, strong and black," Fargo said.

"You're getting on my nerves, big man," the madam muttered, hands on her ample hips.

"I can do better if I put my mind to it," Fargo growled, and the madam suddenly met eyes as cold as ice. A woman who had long ago learned how to separate the men from the boys, Dolly quickly took the measure of the big man in front of her and called to an elderly waiter. She barked orders, and the man disappeared into a back room to return in minutes carrying a big, heavy, gray-enameled coffeepot, chipped, dented but still stout and serviceable.

"It holds seven cups," Dolly said. "That'll be twenty-five cents for the coffee and fifty cents for the pot."

Fargo paid the woman and carried the heavy coffeepot across the room and outside where he retraced his steps back toward the old lumberyard. He halted beside a watering trough, set the pot underneath it, and hurried on. At the old lumberyard he found Ed Whiddle in a drunken stupor, the bottle on the ground beside him all but empty. The man half awoke as Fargo yanked him to his feet. "Wha . . . ?" the man grunted. "Hey, wait," he slurred. Fargo lifted him upright, pushed him against the shed. Whiddle was taller than he'd seemed on the ground, and Fargo watched him blink, trying to focus his blurred eyes. As he began to sink down again Fargo bent over, swung the man over his shoulder, and carried him away.

The man protested drunkenly, belched, his movements aimless resistance as Fargo carried him over his shoulder as if he were a sack of wheat. The Ovaro following, Fargo reached the water trough and dumped Ed Whiddle into it, listening to the man's drunken gasps mingle with the splash of the water. Whiddle surfaced, clutched the edge of the trough with both hands, and tried to pull himself out, but Fargo pressed one big hand atop the man's head and pushed him under water. He held Whiddle there for a minute, and then let him come up gasping for breath. He waited, let Whiddle sputter and spit and mumble drunkenly, then pushed his head under the water again.

When he let Whiddle come up, the man's eyes were open, blinking, wide enough to focus on the big man beside the trough. "What the hell's this?" Whiddle managed as a degree of sobriety returned to him. He half climbed, half fell out of the trough, landing on the ground beside it with a shower of water. He stared up at the big man, his eyes still blurry. "Who're you?" he managed, his words still slurred.

Fargo turned to the Ovaro and took a tin cup out of his saddlebag, brought the heavy enameled coffeepot from under the trough, and poured the strong, black brew. "Drink this," he ordered, and pushed the cup at Ed Whiddle. The man brushed the cup aside with his arm and started to pull himself to his feet.

"Get away from me," he muttered, and half leaned against the trough. He started to move away when Fargo seized his face with one big hand and squeezed, and the man's mouth opened. Fargo poured the coffee into him as Whiddle choked, gasped, spit, and tried to twist away. But Fargo's grip was of iron, and he leaned his body against Ed Whiddle as he continued to force the coffee down the man's throat. Some spilled away, but Whiddle got most of it. Fargo stepped back when the cup was empty and let the man slide to the ground as he poured more coffee. He reached down, pulled Whiddle's head forward, and forced more coffee down his throat. This time Whiddle drank in with less resistance. Fargo poured a third cup when the man finished, poured it into Ed Whiddle, and stepped back as Whiddle, on one knee beside the trough, managed to maintain a sober stare.

"Who're you?" the man gasped out as he wiped his face dry with the sleeve of his shirt. "And what the hell's going on?"

"Name's Fargo," the Trailsman said.

"What do you want with me, mister?" Ed Whiddle frowned, belched, and hiccoughed.

"Some answers about the wagon train that pulled out a few days ago," Fargo said.

Ed Whiddle's jowls seemed to hang down farther into his neck. "I don't know anything," he muttered.

"You were hired on as wheelwright," Fargo reminded him.

"So what? I don't know anything more," the man said sullenly.

"They were supposed to wait for me. Why'd they suddenly pull out?" Fargo questioned.

The man's face stayed sullen, his eyes averted. "Ask them, not me," he muttered, and Fargo saw his hands shake as he pulled himself to his feet.

"I'm asking you," Fargo said.

"I told you, I don't know anything," Whiddle said.

"Try again. You had to hear something, a reason, a decision, something," Fargo insisted.

"I need another cup of coffee," Ed Whiddle said, and reached for the coffeepot. His hand still shook as he filled the cup, Fargo noted, and he started to turn his glance away when the man's hand jerked upward and the still-hot coffee sprayed through the air. Instinctively Fargo shut his eyes and turned away, but he felt the sharp pain as the hot brew splattered the side of his face. He winced, his eyes still shut, when the heavy enameled coffeepot crashed onto the top of his head. Purple and yellow lights flashed in his brain as he fell forward, and the edge of the water trough added another blow as he hit it. He lay on the ground and drew on anger to fight off the gray curtain of unconsciousness that tried to descend over him. He mumbled curses, dug his fingers into the ground, and managed to shake his head. The gray curtain wavered, and he shook his head again and slumped forward to lay on the

37

ground. But the grayness began to lift, fall away, with maddening slowness.

When it finally disappeared, Fargo pushed up on both hands again as objects began to take shape, the water trough first, then the heavy coffeepot lying on its side. "Goddamn," Fargo swore as he got to his feet and blinked to clear his eyes. Whiddle had run and left a trail of wet footprints behind him.

The Trailsman climbed onto the Ovaro and began to follow the tracks as he cursed the sliver of a moon. But the soggy footprints were easy enough to pick up, and he saw that Ed Whiddle had run across the open land and into the trees beyond. Fargo slowed when he entered the stand of hackberry and aspen, halted and listened. He heard the sounds of the man as he fled through the trees. Whiddle ran erratically, stumbling, falling, crashing on, and Fargo sent the Ovaro after the sounds in the darkness ahead.

The tree cover thinned some and let the pale moon in enough for him to spy Ed Whiddle's dark shape crashing through the underbrush. He drew the Colt, aimed, and fired a single shot that slammed into the ground a few inches in front of Whiddle. "Hold it right there," Fargo called, and Whiddle came to a halt and slowly turned. Fargo swung from his horse, holstered the Colt, and walked up to the man. He brought up a short, sudden right hook, and Ed Whiddle flew backward, crashing into a tree and sliding down the trunk to sit on the ground. "That's for the coffeepot," Fargo muttered. He waited for Whiddle to come around, and the man finally opened his eyes, blinked, and rubbed his jaw. "What're you hiding, Whiddle?" Fargo questioned.

"Nothin'," the man said as he pushed himself to his feet sullenly.

"Why'd you run just now?" Fargo pressed.

"I don't like being asked questions," Whiddle muttered.

"Why?" Fargo returned.

"Never did. Too many things I don't want to talk about," Whiddle said. "Besides, you could be anybody."

"Such as a marshal?" Fargo said.

"That's right," Whiddle said. "I want the past to stay that way."

"I don't care about your past. I care about now, about the Anderson wagon train. Talk. Why'd they pull out?" Fargo demanded.

"To beat the fall snows," Whiddle answered, and Fargo felt the frown crease his brow.

"They had plenty of time to beat the fall snows," he said.

"They were told different," the man grunted.

"Who told them different?" Fargo questioned.

"Ask Sam Monroe," Whiddle snapped.

"Sam Monroe?" Fargo echoed in astonishment. "What's he got to do with this?"

"He was real good to them. He's the one to ask, not me. Go talk to Sam Monroe," the man said sullenly. "Christ, I need a drink."

Fargo shook off the astonishment and watched Ed Whiddle rub his hands over his face. "You didn't pull out with the wagon train. Why not?" he questioned.

"Changed my mind," the man said, and looked away.

The answer was an evasion, Fargo was certain. Ed Whiddle was very bothered by something. The past or the present? Fargo wondered. He'd seen men who carried the fears of their past around with them forever. Yet Ed Whiddle didn't have the red-veined face of the perpetual drunk. Something didn't fit right about Ed Whiddle's drinking and his fear of questions. But he'd set the man aside for now, Fargo decided. "I'll go see Sam Monroe come morning," he said. "Meanwhile don't think about running out on me again. Next time I might get real mad."

The man grunted. "Don't come asking questions again. I told you all I know," he said, and turned to walk back through the trees. Fargo let him move out of sight before he swung onto the pinto and slowly made his way back to town. A frown clung to him, and he realized he couldn't just accept the strange turn of events without getting some proper answers. When he reached the hotel in town, he took a room on the second floor and began to undress. He stopped midway, took the little letter from his inside jacket pocket, and sat down beside the lamp by the brass bed The careful, almost labored handwriting sprang out at him as he read the short letter again.

Skye Fargo . . .

We are all real happy you're able to take our offer. This here money will seal our agreement. We'll all meet in Ironwood and be waiting there for you first week in September.

Robert Anderson,
Wagon Master

Fargo folded the letter away, satisfied that there was nothing unclear or uncertain in it, and Abigail Snow came into his thoughts. She'd leapt into his mind the moment Whiddle had spoken Sam Monroe's name, one more surprise that had lain in wait for him. Abigail had appeared out of nowhere the first time, and now she had done so again. Indeed the entire trip had turned into a mixture of unexpected turns and strange coincidences. None of which made him happy. Together they made him uneasy. He finished undressing, stretched his long frame out, and enjoyed the comfort of the bed. He welcomed sleep. It ended his wondering whether the morning would bring answers or just more questions.

3

The uneasiness was still with him when he woke and as he slowly washed and dressed. He'd taken a few extra hours to enjoy the luxury of the bed, and the mid-morning sun streamed through the lone window of the room. Downstairs he found coffee and biscuits, had a cup of the good, bracing liquid, and finished the last of a biscuit as he swung himself onto the Ovaro outside.

He rode slowly on through the remainder of Ironwood and had almost reached the end of town when he came upon the sprawling frame building. A splintered sign carried the name SAM'S SUPPLY AND TRADING COMPANY. He noted two square warehouses that partially flanked the main building, and a line of fenced corrals stretched out in the rear. Sam Monroe had himself a fair-sized operation, it appeared. Two men came from the store carrying sacks of grain and deposited them into a Studebaker Slat Wagon as Fargo dismounted and walked into the building.

He entered a large room jammed full of boxes, crates, barrels, and sacks. A quick survey showed wheat, corn, potatoes, bolts of wool and linen, tobacco and sugar, piles of hides, and an entire corner of tools and shovels. A man appeared from behind a tall wooden crate. He had a coarse face, heavy nose and lips, deep lines along his cheeks, and gray, hard eyes that were shrewdly appraising. A big man, he had huge hands and thick shoulders, but the lower part of his frame grew narrow. "Sam Monroe. What can I do for you, mister," he said in a raspy, abrupt tone.

"Answer me some questions. The name's Fargo," the Trailsman said, and caught the quick flash of surprise in the man's hard eyes.

"I heard of you," Sam Monroe said.

"Expect you have. I hear you can tell me why the Anderson wagon train pulled out without waiting for me," Fargo said.

"Who told you that?" the man challenged.

"Ed Whiddle," Fargo said, and the name drew a sneer from Sam Monroe.

"He's nothin' but a damn windbag," Sam Monroe said.

"They moved out without waiting for me. They were told they had to pull out to avoid the early snows. You tell them that?" Fargo asked, his lake-blue eyes hard.

"They were outfitting with me. I gave them advice. Nothin' more than bein' neighborly," the man answered.

"That's crazy advice. They'd lots of time before the first snows." Fargo frowned.

Sam Monroe's coarse face seemed to grow coarser as a vein throbbed in his temple. "I live here, Fargo. I know what I'm talking about. The snows come early here," he said.

"Not this damn early. This isn't my first visit out here. They had time for me to get them across the Sapphire range and set up on the other side," Fargo insisted.

"You saying I gave them bad advice?" Sam Monroe challenged, and thrust his jaw out belligerently.

"Bad or stupid, comes out the same way," Fargo said evenly.

Monroe pulled his jaw back. "I called it the way I saw it," he growled.

"What else did you do?" Fargo pressed.

"Meaning what?" Monroe frowned back.

"Ed Whiddle said you were real good to them. What'd he mean?" Fargo questioned.

"Whiddle's a big-mouth liar," the man burst out angrily.

"They wouldn't have gone on without somebody to break trail for them. That's why they hired me," Fargo said.

Sam Monroe half shrugged. "When they decided to take my advice, they told me about needing someone to ride trail for them. I got them somebody. Zeke Marston. He knows this country."

"Real lucky he was around, wasn't it?" Fargo commented.

"You hinting at something, Fargo?" the man flared.

"I'm saying something stinks," Fargo said.

"Look, Fargo, Anderson told me they paid you a binder. The money's yours for doing nothing. You can just go and enjoy yourself—" the man said.

The voice cut in sharply. "He can go look for

44

Bobby now," it said, and Fargo turned to see Abigail. "I was passing and saw the Ovaro outside. There's only one horse like that, so I knew you had to be in here," she explained.

Sam Monroe's outburst took him by surprise. "Why don't you mind your own goddamn business, Abigail?" the man shouted. She speared him with a disdainful stare, and he turned to Fargo. "Seems Abigail's been talking to you," he growled. "Well, I'm not having my wife go running off on a wild-goose chase. The boy's dead or past saving by now."

"Can't ever be sure what the Sioux will do," Fargo said.

"I'm sure of that. He's dead, and that's all there is to it. Sheila's not going off when I need her here. She knows she has to take care of the cattle Dan Whitsand's bringing in," Monroe insisted, and flung an angry stare at Abigail. She turned, walked to the door, and waited.

"Are you coming?" she asked Fargo.

"Guess so," he answered, and moved after her.

"You listen here, Fargo. You're not taking my wife off looking for that boy. I won't stand for that. You hear me, Fargo? You just get on your way out of here." Monroe half snarled.

"You giving advice again?" Fargo said evenly. He followed Abigail outside and heard Sam Monroe's curse. Abigail spun to face him, her direct brown eyes shining with something close to triumph. "Don't go running off with the bit," he growled at her.

Her face fell. "Why not? You don't have to keep your word anymore. They've gone off without you. It's sort of as if fate stepped in."

"It's sort of damn strange, that's what," Fargo bit out.

"Maybe, but you can go find Bobby now," she said.

"I've got to think some. I might just have to go find a wagon train," he said.

"Why, dammit," Abigail flared. "They went off without you. They took Sam's advice, good or bad. You've no obligation now."

"If that's all it was," Fargo murmured. "This whole thing comes together real strange."

"It can't be connected with the Sioux and Bobby," she said.

"No, I can't see how or why," he agreed. "But I want to think a few things out first."

"Dammit, what about Bobby?" she pushed at him.

"I'll tell you come morning. I'll stop by," he said.

She glowered back. "You've no excuse now except being a damn coward," she threw at him.

"That's a pretty good one." He laughed.

She swung onto the brown mare and cantered away, leaving a trail of sparks behind her. Fargo took his horse and rode out of Ironwood toward the tall peaks of the Sapphire Mountains to the northwest. He rode casually, slowly, letting the clean winds blow across his furrowed brow as though they could blow away his confusion. He wasn't being given the full story about the wagon train, he was convinced. It had to have been more than just Sam Monroe's advice to make them pull out, he was certain. He had to have added more. It almost seemed as though they'd been sent off, pressured into pulling out. But why? All to give this Zeke Marston a job?

Fargo turned the thought in his mind. Maybe Monroe owed the man a favor. Getting him a wagon train to take over the mountains for good money might have been payment. It was entirely possible. Fargo grimaced as Abigail and the little captured boy swam into his thoughts. The only connection he could see was that Sam Monroe happened to be involved in both incidents. The world was full of strange coincidences, he realized, and he slowed the Ovaro to a halt as the land began to rise up into the foothills of the great mountain range. He spied a wide passage moving upward through the foothills. The wagon train would surely have taken it as far as it went, and he felt the passage beckon to him. But he held back. There were still questions that needed answers.

If Anderson and the others had simply been too quick to swallow Monroe's advice, then to hell with them, Fargo muttered inwardly. He wasn't one for dealing with fools. But there were victims and there were fools. He had to find out which they were before deciding his next move. It was time for another visit with Ed Whiddle, and this time there'd be no more evasions. He turned the Ovaro around and started back toward Ironwood as he wondered how long it would take him to sober the man up this time. Right now Ed Whiddle was the key. Sam Monroe had angrily called Ed Whiddle a liar and a windbag, but he hadn't called him a drunk. Maybe that omission meant something.

Fargo sent the Ovaro into a trot as he realized that the ride to the foothills had been longer than it seemed. The sun was beginning to slide toward the horizon, and he concentrated on making time. The day still held on as he reached town and pulled up in front of the saloon. There was a handful of customers inside and a small crew sweeping the floor and cleaning off tables. Dolly appeared out of a back room as he entered, and her fleshy face fell into an instant scowl. "You again," she muttered. "He's not here. He came in at noon for his first bottle."

Fargo slid words at her carefully. "He's really the town drunk, isn't he?" he remarked.

"Seems like he's got his mind set on becoming that," Dolly said.

"Meaning exactly what?" Fargo asked casually.

"He wasn't even a regular customer until about a week back," the madam said, and Fargo kept the grim smile inside himself. As he'd begun to suspect, Whiddle's nonstop drinking was recent. That's why Sam Monroe hadn't damned him as a drunk. He'd only been one since the wagon train pulled out.

"See you around," Fargo said to the woman as he left, hurried outside, and climbed onto the Ovaro. He made his way around the wagons and pack-mules that crowded the town and reached the old lumberyard. Daylight didn't change the deserted look of the place, and he rode around to the other side of the sagging shed. But the drunken, paunchy figure of Ed Whiddle wasn't slumped against the shed. Fargo dismounted, a stab of apprehension shooting through him at once. Drunks, even new ones, didn't change patterns. They found a place to hole up that suited them and stayed with it. Fargo saw a closed door to the shed and started toward it when the object on the ground caught his eye. He bent down and picked up the bottle. "Goddamn," he swore. The bottle was half full, and no drunk ever left a half full bottle on his own.

Fargo's eyes swept the ground nearby. At once he spotted the hoofprints. He crouched down to examine them. Two horses, one set of prints digging deeper into the ground, the horse carrying a heavier load. An extra rider, Fargo grunted, swore under his breath again, and returned to the Ovaro. He swung after the tracks of the two horses. The prints were not more than a few hours old, he estimated. The tracks moved across the open land, into the trees, and quickly turned up to the higher ridge land. They had slowed as they pulled up steep slopes, the hoofprints drawing closer to each other, and he followed with a sinking feeling inside himself. They hadn't taken Ed Whiddle all this far just to sober him up. Fargo hurried the Ovaro up a sharp incline and reached the top of a ridge. The tracks showed that the two riders had moved along the ridge that suddenly grew rocky, and Fargo drew to a halt as he saw a deep chasm appear. The ravine cut across the ridge at right angles, and Fargo saw the hoofmarks at the edge of it. They had halted, and he saw the tracks move on down the slope and away from the ravine.

Fargo dismounted and stepped to the edge of the chasm. "Shit," he muttered as he stared down at Ed Whiddle's body lying on the rocky bottom of the narrow ravine, grotesquely spread-eagled in death, his right temple soaked in blood where he'd smashed into the rocks. He'd been brought here and thrown to his death, probably still too drunk to know what was happening to him. If he was found, there'd be no bullet holes in him, nothing to suggest he hadn't just wandered off and fallen on his own.

Fargo swore again, at himself this time, for not having pressed Ed Whiddle harder when he'd had him that first time. Dusk had come down, he noted, as he sent the pinto back the way he'd come, the night only a few minutes away. But he rode slowly in the gathering dark and let his thoughts take shape. There was damn little he could piece together yet, but a few things had become clear. Ed Whiddle had stayed back when the wagon train pulled out, and he'd drunk himself into a stupor every day since. There had to be a connection, something Ed Whiddle couldn't live with sober. And whatever it was, somebody made sure he wouldn't talk about it.

Sam Monroe leapt into his mind, and he wondered where the man fitted into the picture. If Monroe had done nothing more than give bad advice, then who wanted Ed Whiddle silenced? And why? Fargo's thoughts turned to the little boy taken by the Sioux. He could see no connection there, either. But Sam Monroe was quickly becoming a figure of strange shadows, quick to give bad advice and quick to write off the boy. A strange man indeed.

Night had settled over the land as Fargo rode back toward Ironwood. He drew back his lips in distaste. A simple job of trail-breaking had turned into a succession of strange events that left a sour taste in his mouth and a growing anger in his gut. He'd come out here to lead a wagon train of simple settlers, and instead he'd been shot at, damn near killed, badgered and lied to, and he'd be damned if he'd just ride away without some real answers.

He finally reached town, tethered the pinto outside the hotel, and went up to his room on the second floor. He hurried down the dim hallway and was about to reach for the doorknob when he glimpsed the thin edge of yellow light from under the door. The big Colt leapt into his hand immediately, and he reached for the doorknob again, slowly and quietly this time. He let the room take shape in his mind. It was small, square, the lone window almost opposite the door across the room. There was no place to hide inside. He closed his hand around the doorknob and turned it slowly, a fraction of an inch, until he heard the latch release. He stepped back and kicked the door open with all the strength of his powerful leg. He half leaped into the room as the door flew open, the big Colt in his hand ready to cut down anyone inside. He halted and heard the hiss of surprise that escaped him as he saw the direct brown eyes gazing at him.

"*You!*" he exploded. "Goddamn, you almost got your pretty little head blown off."

"Almost is almost," she said tartly.

"How'd you get in here?" he asked.

"I told the desk clerk you expected me. He was quick to fill in the rest," she said disdainfully.

"I told you I'd stop by come morning. What are you doing here?" Fargo asked gruffly.

"Sheila's coming to visit you. I wanted to talk to you first," Abigail said. Fargo closed the door and sat down at the edge of the bed.

"Why?"

"Sheila wants to talk to you herself. She wants to ask you herself to find Bobby," Abigail said. "She's very upset, distraught. She'll try anything to get help. I know my sister—"

"What're you trying to say?" Fargo interrupted.

"I'm saying, in the state she's in she's an easy mark. She's too upset to think clearly. All she wants is Bobby found," Abigail said, a warning note in her voice.

"You always this protective? She your kid sister?" Fargo asked.

"Fact is, Sheila's older than I am. We're very different. Sheila has her own ways of dealing with her problems," Abigail said.

"Ways you don't approve of," Fargo supplied.

Abigail's eyes grew darker as her voice flared. "I try to see that she's not used. That's why I came here first. She's desperate, terribly upset. I don't want you taking advantage of her. You just turn away from whatever she offers you."

"You through?" Fargo questioned.

"No, you take advantage of her and you'll pay for it," Abigail threatened.

"How?" Fargo asked mildly.

"I'll think of something. I'll find a way," Abigail snapped.

"You've said your piece. Now you can go," Fargo said gruffly.

Abigail spun on her heel and paused at the door to look back at him. "You still coming by in the morning?" she asked, and suddenly she was very much a young girl.

"That's what I said. I keep my word," he reminded her coldly, and Abigail's lips tightened as she pulled the door open and stalked out. He watched her narrow figure go down the dim hallway, her tight little rear moving primly. He kicked the door shut, pulled off his jacket and shirt, and stretched out across the bed. He'd made his decisions, and visits and pleas wouldn't cut any ice. A surge of irritation went through him. He closed his eyes and let himself doze. He guessed that a little more than a half hour had gone by when he heard the knock at the door—firm, quick taps.

"Come in," he called as he swung from the bed, his eyes on the door and one hand on the butt of the Colt in its holster.

The door opened, and his brows lifted at the sight of the woman who stepped into the room. She had the same color hair as Abigail, but everything else was different. Perhaps ten years older, he guessed. She was bigger and heavier with deep, pillowy breasts that pressed hard against a scoop-necked white cotton blouse held by a drawstring at the neck. She wore her hair shoulder-length, and her face was heavier, flatter of cheekbone than Abigail's, her nose wider, lips fuller. But most of all, where Abigail gave out primness and severity, Sheila Monroe gave out a dark sultriness. She pushed the door closed behind her, and her eyes stayed on his. "I'm Sheila Monroe," she announced.

"Been expecting you," he said, and saw the moment of real surprise flood her dark eyes.

"You just thought I'd be coming to see you?" she asked, her voice low, almost husky.

"No, I was told you were coming," Fargo said.

Her lips fell open as surprise deepened, and then she pulled them closed with a hiss of exasperation. "Abigail." She sniffed, and he nodded. "Damn that girl," Sheila Monroe said. "I know she means well, but she can be a problem."

"I'll second that," Fargo commented. Sheila Monroe's eyes moved across the muscled, powerful beauty of his shoulders and chest, lifted her glance to linger on the chiseled strength of his face.

"She described you well," Sheila Monroe said.

"How's that?" Fargo frowned.

"Abigail said you were very good-looking, with a raw, animal quality that probably excited many women," Sheila Monroe said.

"I'll bet she turned her nose up when she said it," Fargo commented, and Sheila's wide mouth broke into a half laugh.

"Yes, she did," Sheila agreed. "God, that's the first time I've laughed since Bobby was taken," she added, and drew her face in soberly at once. But her eyes continued to move across the big man in front of her. "She was right, too, I'd wager," she remarked.

"Maybe," Fargo conceded.

Sheila Monroe's dark eyes grew darker as they bored into him. "I've no time left to play games. You know why I've come. I want you to bring Bobby back if he's alive. I've got to know if he is. Abigail told me why you turned her down, and I understood. I was disappointed, but I understood. A man is only as good as his word," she said, and Fargo decided that Sheila was not only older but also a lot wiser than her little sister. "I came now because I'm . . . well, I'm ready to give you anything I can if you'll try to find Bobby," she said pointedly.

"It wouldn't make any difference, honey. I don't make my mind up in bed," Fargo said not ungently.

Sheila's full lips turned into a wry half smile. "I was afraid of that from what I'd heard about you," she said. She added a little half shrug of resignation. "You fight with whatever few weapons you have," she murmured.

"Besides, I couldn't do it even if I'd a mind to." Fargo grinned.

Sheila Monroe frowned at him for a moment. "Abigail," she muttered.

"Only a complete bastard would take advantage of a desperate, upset woman, I was told." Fargo laughed.

Sheila drew a deep sigh. "Abigail doesn't believe in certain things. Besides, she really does try to protect me from myself," the woman said, and her eyes peered hard at the big man. "But as you said, you don't make your mind up in bed. It wouldn't have mattered any."

" 'Fraid not," he agreed.

"In fact, you have your mind made up already, haven't you?" Sheila said, her eyes probing into him.

"Could be," he told her.

Sheila Monroe's dark eyes stayed on him for a long moment, probing, searching his face, and he saw the tiny, wry smile touch the corners of her lips. "Good," she said.

"Good?" Fargo frowned.

Sheila Monroe's hand came up, and her fingers pulled the drawstring at the scooped neck of the blouse. The neckline fell open wide, and the tops of her deep, pillowy breasts spilled outward as if anxious to come free. She met the question in Fargo's lake-blue eyes. "No bargains, no trading off, no deals. Now I can do it just because I want to," she said.

"Where does Sam Monroe fit in?" Fargo asked.

"I needed a home, three meals a day, and some roots for Bobby. Sam Monroe needed someone to help him keep account of his business. We made an agreement," the woman said.

"A marriage of convenience, they call it," Fargo remarked.

"Exactly," Sheila agreed. "It was understood there'd be nothing more unless it came about on its own. It never did; two years now, and it's stayed a marriage of convenience. It will never be more." She wriggled her shoulders, the loosened blouse fell from her shoulders, and she stood before him with the deep, full, heavy breasts proudly thrust forward, large pink-brown nipples set in pink circles, a woman's breasts just managing to avoid matronliness.

"Why me? Why now?" Fargo asked.

"If I'm not still trying to reach you?" The woman smiled almost sadly. "Because I'm tired doing without. Because I don't think anyone such as you will be crossing my way again. Because I need to forget the world for a little while, and I look at you and know you can make that happen."

"I'll sure as hell try, Sheila Monroe. Those are good enough reasons," Fargo said, and began to shed clothes. Sheila undid the black skirt, let it fall away, and pushed the half-slip down to stand naked before him. She had wide hips, thighs a little heavy, a little belly carrying a few pounds too much, and beneath it a convex little pubic mound decorated by a surprisingly small tuft of curly, black nap. But Sheila still managed to avoid matronliness. In fact, she had a very womanly, earthy desirability to her, and he felt himself growing, rising, his groin responding to the waiting, naked beckoning of her body. He shed the last of his clothes and saw Sheila's eyes focus on the powerful, full symbol of pleasure that thrust toward her. Her lips fell open as she stared, and he reached out to pull her to him.

She came at once, her skin hot and soft against him, and he heard her gasp as his organ pushed against the inner part of her thighs.

"Oh . . . oh," she murmured, and her hands tightened around him. The large, deep breasts pushed sweet softness against him, and as he sank down on the bed with her, his mouth encircled one full, brown-pink nipple. He drew on it, his tongue caressing, his lips drawing the end of the big breast up into his mouth. "Oh . . . oh, oh. It's been too long," Sheila muttered, and he pressed his face into the downy softness of the deep breasts, sweet smothering that enveloped him with its smooth heat. He rolled his face in their softness, found a large tip, and pulled on it, and Sheila Monroe cried out with pleasure. His hand moved down to stroke the smooth skin below her breasts, wandered farther, and pressed into the convex little belly, dropped down to rest against the fleshy little pubic mound. As his palm pressed down on the curly, black tuft he could feel the warm wetness of her below as Sheila's full-fleshed thighs fell open and her ample hips lifted.

"Oh, Fargo . . . oh, please, oh, please," she whispered, and her arm wrapped around his neck to keep his face against her breasts. He moved his fingers downward farther, down to the edge of her wet, warm lubricious lips, and she cried out in anxious delight as a quiver went through her body. He touched her slowly, drawing his fingers across the tiny, sensitive lips, and Sheila's gasped scream was a shuddering sound. He pulled his face from the pillowed breasts and traced a simmering little pathway with his lips down across her abdomen and the fleshy little belly. Sheila's hips lifted her body again, and he heard her half whimpered plea. "Fargo . . . Fargo. . . . Please, please."

He turned, brought his throbbing maleness over her, and let it slap against the fleshy little pubic mound. Sheila heaved, her hips thrust upward, and she let out a throaty cry. Her hand came down, wildly sought for him, and curled around the pulsating warmth of him, and she half sobbed in delight. Sheila murmured, pulled on him, and let her legs fall open as she tried to bring him over her. He half lifted her, and she wriggled herself under him. As he lowered himself over her round little belly she cried out in protest. "Please, please, don't make me wait," she begged.

Fargo moved down, slid along the curly, black tuft that tickled against him, and as if with a vision of its own, his organ found her waiting, warm funnel. He probed, touched, and pressed deeper, and Sheila's throaty cries gathered strength. Fargo paused, let her gasped entreaties rise, plunged forward, and Sheila's fleshy thighs pressed around him and her little belly rose, jiggled, quivered, as she gave out tiny half screams of delight.

She cried out a breathless litany of pleasure, and the deep, heavy breasts lifted to push against him. Her ample hips lifted, pushed upward to match his every thrust, and Sheila's lips stayed open as a low, guttural moan came from her, a singsong paean of delight that came from deep inside her. "More, Fargo. It's been so long. I can't . . . I can't make it, help me, help me," Sheila cried out, sudden panic in her voice.

"You'll make it, honey," Fargo murmured, drew back almost to the tip of the dark, damp channel, and Sheila screamed.

"No, don't leave . . . don't leave," she cried out, and he held there, waited, and felt her shudder, her desire building as panic urged it on. She began to quiver, her quiverings growing stronger, becoming a deep shudder that coursed through her, and he felt her thighs grow tight around him. "*Fargo!*" Sheila screamed as the moment of ecstasy began to surge through her, rise, grow stronger, envelop, encompass all feeling. "Yes, yes, I'm coming . . . oh, yes," she cried out, and her screams rose as he plunged deep into her and exploded with her. Sheila lifted, her belly quaking against his hard-muscled body, her arms pulling his head down onto the pillowy breasts that shook as she climaxed, and the throaty cry tore out from deep inside her.

He stayed with her, pumping into her, extending ecstasy to the limits of pleasure, and he finally heard the deep rush of breath that came from her as she fell back, thighs loosening from around him, her legs falling away, her arms dropping to her sides. Even her breasts seem to deflate and lay flaccidly under his chest. He rolled over and lay beside her and listened to her heaving gasps of breath that finally lessened to a soft, hissing sound. He felt her hand reach out, find his, and press his fingers over the little pubic mound. She held him there, her hand over his until finally she half turned, leaned over him, one deep breast draped over his chest, a pillow of soft flesh.

"You did it," she said, almost awe in her voice. "I didn't think it could be done."

"Make you come?" he asked.

"That, too, but mostly make me forget everything for a few wonderful moments," Sheila said. She pushed herself to a sitting position and began to pull on clothes. He watched her movements, slow, tired, the body echoing the disconsolateness of the spirit. "You'll do whatever you think you have to do. I know that," she said. "I'm glad I came."

He swung from the bed as she rose and moved to the door. She paused to press her mouth on his for another long moment, then pulled back and left quickly. No last-minute appeals, no soft words. Sheila had her own set of principles, an unusual woman, he decided, not afraid to give and not afraid to take, willing to offer and willing to understand. She deserved a better deal from life. He grunted as he lay down across the bed. He let sleep come to him with the cool night wind that drifted in through the window. His mind had been made up. Nothing had changed.

Morning came bright and crisp. When he finished dressing, he spent some time getting the trail dust out of the Ovaro's coat with a body brush and curry. When he finished, he headed the glistening black-and-white steed through town. Passing Sam Monroe's store and warehouses, he rode on until he halted at a low-roofed ranch house. He saw a hog pen with a half dozen small pigs in it just off to one side at the front of the house, a small barn behind the pen. As he dismounted he saw Abigail come out of the house. She strode toward him, and he watched her draw near, noticing the fury in her direct, brown eyes. She strode toward him, didn't slow, never broke her stride as she brought the blow up sharply from her side. He managed to duck, and the blow only grazed his face.

"What the hell's wrong with you?" Fargo frowned as he avoided another roundhouse swing.

"Bastard. Stinking, unprincipled bastard," Abigail flung at him. "You had to do it. You had to take advantage of her."

"You don't jump to conclusions, do you, honey? You take a flying nosedive," Fargo returned.

"Don't you lie to me. I know what happened. She traded herself for your help, and you took her up on it. You slept with her," Abigail accused.

"Sheila tell you that?" Fargo questioned.

"She didn't have to. We lived together a long time. When Sheila's been . . . been . . . ?"

"Screwed?" Fargo supplied, and drew a furious glare.

"When she's been to bed with someone, I always have to wake her the next morning. She just stays curled up until she's awakened," Abigail told him.

"It's called being satisfied," Fargo remarked.

Fargo's glance flicked past Abigail and saw Sheila stepping out of the house. "After I told you how upset she was," Abigail threw at him, and he brought his eyes back to her, "after I told you not to take advantage of her. How could you do that?" she said.

"It was easy, just as easy as this," Fargo bit out as he bent down and wrapped his arms around Abigail's knees. He hoisted her over his shoulder, and she screamed in protest.

"You let me down, damn you," she demanded.

Fargo took a half dozen steps forward. "Sure thing, honey," he said as he tossed her over the fence and into the hog pen. She landed in the slops, which splashed into her face.

"Oh, damn," Abigail snorted. "Oh, you rotten

bastard." Abigail started to pull herself up, slipped in the mud and slops, and slid facedown across the ground. Fargo turned to Sheila as she halted beside him.

"Don't tell me. I can guess," she said.

"I just had enough of her damn ranting and raving," Fargo said mildly. "She really flies off half cocked, doesn't she?"

"I apologize," Sheila said, and Fargo saw Abigail pull her mud and slop-covered body up along one of the rails of the pen. She sputtered oaths and frowned at Sheila from a face half covered with mud.

"Why are you apologizing to this . . . this *lecher*?" she spit out.

"Abigail, be quiet for once in your young life," Sheila said sternly, and her eyes turned to Fargo, anxiousness in their dark depths.

"I'll try to find the boy for you," he said. "I've some questions for that wagon train, too, but I won't be breaking trail for them. I'll be able to look for the boy."

Sheila leaned her head against his chest, the big breasts as soft and pillowy as he remembered. "Come with me while I tell Sam," she said, and he nodded. He saw Abigail climbing through the rails of the hog pen, part of her face clean enough for him to see her frowning stare. "You follow me, Abigail," Sheila snapped, and strode back to the house as Abigail tagged along.

Fargo turned away and leaned against the top of the pen as he waited. He had some questions readied for Sheila, but it was Abigail who emerged from the house first, wearing a clean, brown-checked shirt and skirt. She glowered as she halted in front of him.

"Sheila says I owe you an apology," Abigail muttered. "She said it wasn't the way I thought."

"Only you're not sure of that," Fargo said.

"That's right," she flared at once. "Maybe you're just more clever than most."

"Maybe," he agreed. "And maybe you're just more stiff-backed than most."

"I'm not stiff-backed," Abigail snapped. "I still say you didn't have to. Ever hear of declining?"

"I'll take reclining over declining any day," Fargo said. "You ought to try it."

Abigail snapped her head away from him as Sheila came from the house, hurried into the barn, and drove out in a dark green buckboard. "Let's go," she said, and Abigail climbed in to sit beside her as Fargo pulled the Ovaro alongside the rig.

"How did the Sioux capture Bobby?" he asked. "Was he aboard a stage or at a house they raided?"

"He was with me, right here," Sheila said. "We'd just brought groceries back from town. I was unloading, and Bobby had gone off not more than a dozen yards away when they charged out of the trees. Eight of them, the leader a Sioux with a huge barrel chest. They just scooped up Bobby and took off with him. I can still hear him screaming."

Fargo's brows came together in a frown as he turned Sheila's words in his mind. "Just raced out, took the boy, and made off with him," he echoed, and Sheila nodded. "Damn strange," he thought aloud. "Not the usual Sioux tactic." Sheila and Abigail both turned waiting glances his way. "When the Sioux raid, they usually kill anybody on hand. They pillage and, most times, set the torch to whatever's left. Yet these only grabbed Bobby and ran," he explained.

"It seemed as though Bobby was all they'd come for," Abigail interjected. "But why?"

"Damn strange," Fargo muttered. "They carry off any other youngsters around here?" he asked Sheila.

"Not that I heard about," she told him, and he grimaced.

"Strange, all right, but the Sioux are full of surprises," Fargo said. "They have their reasons for whatever they do." He held back on setting out some of those reasons. They went from bad to sickening, and it'd do Sheila no good to know them all. But the taking of the boy had been unusual, especially in the way it'd been done. The whole thing only added to the uneasy feeling that lay inside him.

Sam Monroe's supply store came into view, and Sheila pulled the buckboard to one side of the entrance and stepped down with Abigail at her side. Fargo followed them both into the store and saw Sam Monroe's eyes grow hard as he came from a back room to see Sheila. He glanced at Abigail and Fargo, then returned his gaze to Sheila. "What's all this?" he rasped.

"Fargo's agreed to look for Bobby," Sheila said, and Fargo watched Sam Monroe's face grow tight at once, a slow flush of anger creeping across his cheeks.

"Not on my money, he isn't," the man bit out.

"I'm paying him out of my own savings," Sheila said.

The man's face thrust forward at her. "You're

not goin' chasin' off on this damnfool thing, not at this time of the year," he thundered.

"I want to find my boy. I've got to know what's happened to him," Sheila said firmly.

"He's dead. The damn Indians killed him, that's what happened to him," Monroe shouted.

"I have to know," Sheila said with quiet doggedness.

"Goddammit, I need you here, and this is where you're going to stay," the man returned.

"You're a selfish, callous ox, Sam Monroe," Fargo heard Abigail cut in, and Sam Monroe whirled on her.

"You stay the hell out of this and shut up," he roared, and Fargo caught Sheila's glance.

"I'll wait outside," Fargo said. He started to turn, then took hold of Abigail's wrist. "You too," he said.

"No," Abigail started to say, but he had yanked her outside with him before she could protest any further. "Damn you," she snapped as he released her wrist.

"Sheila can handle it best on her own," he told her. "Besides, you can keep me company."

"A lot you care about that," Abigail glowered, glancing back at the store. He saw both concern and anger in her face. "I can't understand a man being so callous," she muttered as the sounds of arguing drifted from inside the store, Monroe roaring, Sheila quietly insistent. When Sheila strode from the store a few minutes later, Sam Monroe was right behind her. His angry eyes found Fargo at once.

"You're just taking her money for nothin', and you know it," he accused.

"I don't see that's any of your damn business," Fargo said calmly.

"You're not taking her out chasing through the mountains, you hear me?" the man said. Fargo met his furious glare with unmoving calm, and Sam Monroe took a step closer to him, his fists clenched at his sides, rage flooding his heavy face. "Why don't you just go on your damn way and stay the hell out of this?" the man demanded.

"Couldn't do that anymore." Fargo smiled pleasantly. "It's kind of got my curiosity going." Sam Monroe sputtered, but he caught the steel just beneath the pleasant smile and backed away.

"Then go on, you damn fool. You might as well try to find a needle in a haystack," the man said, spun on his heel, and stalked back into the store. Fargo glimpsed three men watching from the corrals and the warehouses, saw them move away as Monroe left. He swung onto the Ovaro and brought the horse alongside the buckboard where Sheila sat with Abigail.

"I'll find him," Fargo told her. "I'll sure try my best."

Sheila's dark eyes met his searching glance. "I can't ask more," she said, her face set and expressionless. He glanced at Abigail and saw that her brown eyes were very round and full of hope.

"I know Bobby's alive. I feel it inside," she said. He nodded, accepting the remark with no reservations. He wouldn't take it as gospel, but he wouldn't discard it, either. He'd come to know better than that. The years had taught him that the heart had its own wisdoms.

He touched the brim of his hat as he set the pinto into a canter and rode northwest to where the purple peaks of the Sapphire Mountains waited. He thought about Sam Monroe's last outburst as he rode. To most men it would seem an impossible task to find a crazy Sioux with a little boy; indeed, as impossible as finding the needle in the haystack. But they didn't know the ways of the Indian. The Sioux, like all the tribes, behaved out of their built-in patterns. Even when they did the unusual, such as kidnapping Bobby—Fargo frowned—they didn't just vanish into the air. They left signs, trails, but more important, they'd follow their pattern of behavior. They had struck, taken little Bobby, for whatever their reasons were. But they'd not simply retire. They'd hit again if they could. The Sioux didn't make isolated raids. They were always part of a pattern—always.

He rode steadily as his thoughts took shape, and when he reached the wide passage that started through the mountain foothills, he sent the pinto up its broad slope. He'd gone more than halfway up the hill when he found the wagon tracks overlapping each other. There were enough of them to indicate eight wagons. He followed the marks of the wide wheels. The broad passage began to narrow and soon was barely wide enough to accommodate the wide Conestogas. Heavy tree cover crowded the road on both sides, mostly shadbush and black oak, and the wheel marks were pressed into the very edges of the pathway. He drew to a halt where the path ended, and he saw where they had used axes to hack their way through high, thick brush. They had cut their way almost at right angles to where the path had been. High plains land visible in the distance was their goal. Fargo grunted disapprovingly. Zeke Marston wasn't much of a trailbreaker, he decided. A line of Rocky Mountain maple with wide spaces between ran only a dozen yards below.

Fargo turned the pinto and followed along the path that had been hacked out of the thick brush. He halted at a spot where it rose over a little ridge of land, and he lifted himself in the saddle. His eyes swept the foothills he had just climbed. His quick scan picked up the thin cloud of dust as it spiraled up from the hills below. Not more than one or two riders, he murmured silently, and he moved from the passageway into the heavy, tall brush that lined the sides of the path. The dense brush made moving forward a slow process, but his eyes swept the thick foliage as he pushed his way through. He finally spotted what he searched to find. A line of brush appeared to his right with half broken and bruised ends, the mark of a single horse moving through just as he did now. Three days old, he guessed by the amount of dried and hardened sap on the broken brush ends. "Unshod Indian pony," he muttered as he peered down at the thick grass that covered the ground, the blades flattened and pressed down but not torn and broken as a horse with shoes would have left them.

He continued on, keeping in the thick brush as he watched the thin line of dust move along the pathway toward him. He pushed on to where the heavy brush still leaned half across the passage. He halted, waited, and saw the thin spiral of dust vanish as the ground became mostly grass and weed. The sound of horses moving fast came to him as he waited, and he drew the big Sharps from its saddle holster. He had the rifle aimed and ready to fire as two horses came into sight. "Goddamn," Fargo muttered, and pushed the Ovaro out of the thick brush, his eyes hard as he saw Sheila and Abigail rein to a halt. He lowered the rifle as he speared them with his eyes. "What are you doing here?" he growled.

"Looking for you," Sheila said.

"Why?" Fargo said.

"To go find Bobby with you," Sheila said. "I decided the hell with arguing anymore with Sam."

"I'm not dragging you two along. This is no guided tour," Fargo said.

"I know it'll be dangerous, but I can't stay home. I'll go crazy waiting and wondering," Sheila replied.

"You managed up to now. You'll have to keep on," Fargo said.

"If Bobby's alive, he's scared out of his mind. If he's grabbed and taken off again, God knows what'll happen to him. A child can take only so much. I want him to see someone he knows," Sheila argued.

Fargo's eyes left her and peered past her as he saw a line of trees shake vigorously. "Stay quiet," he said as he moved the Ovaro beside a tall hackberry. He pulled himself up from the saddle into the tree, climbed higher, and wrapped himself around a thick branch that let him peer over the heavy brush and down the hillside. He glimpsed the riders as they came into sight and disappeared again into the trees. A handful, he saw, riding hard, cutting diagonally across the passage that had been hacked out by the wagon train. Sam Monroe was at the head of the group, and he let his eyes move in a half circle to the terrain close at hand. He scanned the area and let himself slide from the tree and back onto the Ovaro where he met Sheila's dark eyes.

"Your husband's coming with some friends," Fargo said. "They're moving fast."

Sheila frowned in surprise. "I didn't think he'd come after me," she said.

"It's not out of love," Abigail snapped tartly.

"Follow me," Fargo said, and turned the Ovaro into the brush on the other side of the pathway. He pushed his way up an incline to emerge into a place where Sierra juniper grew tall amid a series of vertical rock formations. It wasn't time for a showdown, not without knowing a lot more than he did, Fargo had decided. Sam Monroe might be nothing more than Abigail's description of him—a callous, selfish man. There were still only unanswered questions, and Fargo halted at the rock fissure he'd seen from in the trees. From the ground the junipers obscured the entrance to the rock opening. "You stay in there and be quiet until I get back," he said.

He waited for a moment as Sheila and Abigail began to make their way through the trees and into the fissure, then turned and rode up the north side of the hill and down in a half circle that brought him back to the passageway. He rode noisily and glimpsed the band of riders as they came into view and veered off to go after him. He was halted in a small glen when they reached him, and he saw Sam Monroe's eyes make a quick sweep of the clearing.

"Where is she?" the man snapped.

"Where's who?" Fargo asked mildly.

"You know goddamn well who. Sheila, that's who," Sam Monroe roared.

"How would I know?" Fargo shrugged.

"She took off to go with you. Her and that goddamn Abigail bitch," the man swore.

"You see her around here?" Fargo asked.

The man's eyes swept the glen again, peered into the trees, and returned to Fargo. "She shows up and you better send her the hell back home, Fargo," Monroe flung at the big man.

"You asking me to be impolite?" Fargo said.

"Don't play games with me, Fargo," Monroe growled.

"That goes both ways," Fargo said, the pleasantness disappearing from his voice.

"What's that mean?" Monroe frowned.

"It means something stinks about all of this, Monroe," Fargo shot back harshly. "I don't know where you fit in yet, but I'm going to find out."

"I don't know what you're talking about. You got something to say, say it," Monroe returned.

"When I'm ready," Fargo answered.

Monroe's heavy face drew together darkly. "I've had it with you, Fargo," he half snarled, and Fargo saw the almost imperceptible movement of his hand toward his holster. Fargo drew and fired in a single, lightning-fast motion, and Sam Monroe's hat flew off. The man's hand froze at his side as he stared into the barrel of the big Colt aimed at him.

"I figure the next one ought to get you right between the eyes," Fargo remarked calmly, and flicked a glance to the others. They sat motionless, their eyes filled more with awe than with courage. "It's time to leave, gents," Fargo said, the six-gun still trained on Sam Monroe. "Turn around real slow and move out," he ordered.

Monroe pulled on his horse, wheeled the animal in a half circle, and the others followed. "I'll remember this, Fargo," he called back.

"I hope you will," Fargo said, and kept the Colt ready to fire as the riders moved down the hillside, through the brush, and out of sight. He waited, listened, and finally satisfied that they had continued on, he turned and headed upward to the Juniper Sierra and the rock fissure. Sheila and Abigail rode out slowly when he stopped before the rocks and halted before him. "They're gone," he said. "You can go back the way you came. You'll be safe enough, and you'll make it before dark."

Sheila shook her head. "Bobby has to see somebody he knows. Besides, I've no reason to go back now," she said.

"Yes, you do," Fargo told her. "If I bring Bobby back and it turns out that Sam Monroe's no more than a stupid, greedy ox, you might still want that roof over your head. For a while more, at least— long enough for Bobby to become himself again." He saw Sheila's eyes darken as his words struck home, and he let her wrestle with her thoughts. She finally answered in measured words, her dark eyes lifting to him.

"I'll go back if Abigail stays in my place," she said.

"You don't need to bargain, Sheila," Abigail cut in. "I'll just follow along after him. I can go wherever I want."

"You can get yourself hog-tied too," Fargo grunted, but his eyes stayed with Sheila.

"I'm thinking about Bobby," Sheila said. "Agreed?"

Fargo drew a long sigh. "I want you back there so you can keep an eye on your husband. Agreed?" he said. "Now get moving." He watched Sheila and Abigail embrace quickly, and Sheila paused before him.

"Good luck," she said simply, but he knew the

two words were a hope, a plea, and a prayer. She hurried her horse away, and Fargo turned to Abigail. She set her face with firmness, her eyes bold and challenging.

"Why do I think you're going to be a pain in the ass?" he asked appraisingly.

"Because you're conceited, arrogant, unbending, and rude," she snapped.

"And right," he grunted as he turned the Ovaro.

4

He had pushed through the thick brush to return to the hacked-out passage below, and Abigail came alongside him. "I'll pull my weight," she said firmly. "I can shoot and I can ride. Daddy taught me both."

"Did he, now?" Fargo grunted. "I sure hope so."

"What does that mean?" she asked at once.

"It means you'll have to be looking out for your own neck. I'll have enough to do if we find Bobby," Fargo said.

"I'm perfectly capable of that." Abigail sniffed.

He fastened a brusque glance at her. "You bring any supplies along?" he asked.

"Plenty," she returned with disdain. She didn't stick her tongue out at him, but he was sure she was thinking about it. He turned the pinto onward along the passage as he studied the ground. He picked up the wagon tracks again; they were plain and led to where the passage cut into lush, rolling hills. The thick grass made picking up the marks more difficult, but he found enough to see that the wagons had crossed the first low hill. He rode along in the shadow of the towering mountain peaks until Abigail spurred her horse forward to come abreast of him. He glanced up and saw her frown.

"You're following the damn wagons," she snapped. "You're supposed to be looking for the Sioux."

"That's what I'm doing," he said.

"Hell you are. I can see you following the wagon tracks. Don't you take me for a fool, Skye Fargo," Abigail tossed back in protest.

"I'm trying not to, but you're making it damn hard for me." He sighed as she glared back. He raised his arm, brought it around in a sweeping gesture that took in the vastness of the land that surrounded them with mountains, plateaus, hills and dales, heavy tree growth, and places of tall rock formations. "Pick a spot you'd like me to find the Sioux," he said.

Her lips tightened. "Why'd you say you could do it?" she returned.

"Because I can. But just riding off in all directions isn't the way," he told her. She waited, her eyes softening. "You want to find a chicken hawk, find some chickens," he said. "You want to find a grizzly, find yourself a river full of salmon. I get to the wagons and I'll find the Sioux somewhere nearby. I just hope not too nearby," he added grimly.

Abigail nodded, and her eyes held his. "I'm sorry," she said. "I'm just so anxious and wound up."

Fargo's gaze lifted as the sun dropped behind the tall peaks. He spurred the Ovaro into a canter, rode

75

across the next hillside, and pulled into a cluster of blue spruce at the bottom of a low rise. He dismounted as dusk began to drift across the land. He took a step from the Ovaro, and his eyes narrowed as he caught the faintly acrid, musty, dark odor. Abigail had slid to the ground, and her eyes were on him as he cast a quick glance at her. "Stay right here. Sit down. I'll be back," he said.

"I don't intend to be treated like a child," she snapped, and he saw her nose crinkle. "I smell something strange." She frowned.

"Musk," he said.

"What's that?" she questioned.

"Tell you later. Stay here," he said, and stepped into the trees. He moved carefully, his nostrils flaring as he drew in deep drafts of air. He halted, sniffed hard again, turned slowly, and followed the scent in a half circle. The odor grew stronger as he turned to face a small rise. He started to move upward toward the top of the incline. He heard the snap, the shudder of leaves, and Abigail's scream at the same instant.

"Shit," he swore as he broke into a run. He saw her as he reached the top of the rise. She hung head-down beside a young sapling, her skirt all but covering her face, revealing pink bloomers above long, shapely calves.

The snare, the kind trappers called yank-ups, had her by the ankle, and she dangled, swinging slowly in a circle. "Help me, dammit," she screamed as much in fright and anger as in pain. He drew the narrow, double-edged throwing knife from the holster around his calf and stepped to the rope that held her. He wrapped one arm around her midriff, bare above the upended skirt and the top of the pink bloomers. "What are you doing?" she called out at once.

"Fixing it so you don't fall on your dumb head when I cut the rope," he answered as he held the knife against the snare and severed the rope with one quick swipe of the blade. His arm around her pressed her to him, and he lowered her to the ground. She brought her hands up to pull her skirt down at once, then yelped as she put weight on her ankle. She lay back on her elbows and blinked up at him.

"Too bad Daddy didn't teach you to obey orders," Fargo said coldly.

"How was I supposed to know about that thing?" she asked.

"I told you to stay put," Fargo said.

"What's it doing here, anyway?" she said, ignoring his admonition.

"Waiting to trap whatever steps into it," Fargo said. "Coyote, raccoon, deer, possum, dumb girl."

Abigail's lips tightened into a thin line, but he saw the flicker of apology in her eyes. "Is that what you went off to look for?" she asked.

"Not that especially, but I knew we were near a trap line of some kind. That's why you smelled the musk. That's a concoction made from the scent glands of animals such as otter, beaver, deer, or muskrat. Trappers put it on traps to attract animals," he explained.

She moved and winced. "My ankle hurts most, but I hurt all over. I feel like a rubber band that's been snapped," she said.

"You were lucky. I've seen yank-ups break legs," Fargo said, and moved his hand to her ankle. She gasped in pain as he pressed, and he could feel the ankle swelling. "It needs bandaging," he said.

"I've some in my saddlebag," Abigail answered, and he rose, bent over, and lifted her up and tossed her over his shoulder as though she were a sack of wheat. He heard her murmur in pain as he moved down the hillside to the little glen of spruce. He dumped her on the ground on her rear, and she yelped again. "You don't have to be so rough," she complained.

"Feel like it," he muttered as he strode to her saddlebag. "Next time follow orders. You went off just to show off your damn independence." Her silence was an admission, and he rummaged inside the saddlebag until he found a roll of bandages. He knelt down and began to bandage the ankle as she winced. "You'll be able to hobble around on it come morning, and you can rest it more while you ride," he said.

"Thank you," she said when he finished, sounding chastened. The night turned cool, and he made a small fire and warmed strips of beef jerky. "Would you get my blanket?" Abigail asked when they finished eating. He rose, fetched the blanket and his own bedroll. He began to undress, feeling Abigail's eyes on him as the last of the firelight danced across the muscled smoothness of his chest. He was wearing cut-down BVDs that showed the powerful grace of his thighs and legs, and he halted just short of being naked and turned to her. She looked away instantly.

"You going to sleep all dressed up like that?" he asked her as he slid into his bedroll.

"Would you turn around?" she asked.

"That makes twice," he said. "But I'll go along

with it this time, seeing as how you have a sore ankle." He turned on his side and listened to her little murmurs of discomfort as she turned and twisted to take off clothes sitting down. "Want some help?" he called.

"No, thank you," Abigail said stiffly, and he heard her pull the blanket over her. Maybe she'd learned a lesson, he told himself as he dropped off to sleep. The night stayed quiet, and he slept soundly, to be awakened not only by the morning sun but also by a roar of curses. He sat up as the sound echoed down to the clearing.

"Goddamn bastard. Son of a bitch sprang the yank-up," the voice roared. "Look at the goddamn footprints. Cut my rope, too, goddammit." Fargo's eyes followed the sound to the top of the rise as he pulled on trousers and gun belt. He saw the two figures there, one very tall and very thin, the other medium height. The tall one did the shouting. "Goddamn bastard. I'll kill him," he heard the man swear. Abigail had come awake and was wriggling into the brown-checked shirt. Fargo caught a brief glimpse of smooth, round curves from the side as she threw the shirt on. But the two men on the ridge had turned, spotted them, and he saw the smaller one point.

"Look, Eddie. Down there," the man said, and both started to charge down the hillside. The tall one's long, thin legs came down the slope in a strange, ungainly gait that made him resemble a wounded crane. The man reached the clearing of spruce as Fargo got to his feet. He had a cadaverous face, long and sunken. Dirty, stringy brown hair hung down to his shoulders and formed straggly strands along the sides of his face. But his eyes held

Fargo's gaze, pale blue and glowing with a strange light. The shorter man sported a three-day stubble over a round, oily face with small black eyes.

"You had yourself a meal out of my snare, goddammit," the very tall, thin one snarled as his eyes took in the ashes of the small fire. "What'd you take out of my snare?"

"Nothing you'd caught there. Simmer down," Fargo said.

The tall man's eyes went to Abigail as she got to her feet with her weight mostly on one foot, and Fargo saw the strange light in the man's pale blue eyes grow brighter. "Entertained a lady at my expense, did you now," the man said, and his lips formed a mirthless smile as he devoured Abigail with his eyes.

"No, it was an accident. The lady stepped into it," Fargo said.

The very tall man's cadaverous face stayed on Abigail, the mirthless smile suddenly fixed, and his tongue came out to flick across his lips. "Is that so?" he said without taking his eyes from Abigail. "I got me a real live pussy and you cut her down." He half turned, the pale blue eyes spearing Fargo with their strange light. "That makes her mine, mister," the man said.

"I don't think so," Fargo said evenly, and saw the smaller man move to the side and move away into the clearing in a half circle.

"That's where you're wrong," the very tall one said, the smile becoming a half sneer. "Taking the catch out of a man's trap is stealing under the law, and that's what you did," he said. His quick glance at Abigail was made of anticipation. It was loins, not law, that churned inside him, Fargo knew.

"We were just pulling out. Now you back off and we'll be on our way," Fargo said.

"Not the little lady. She's mine," the tall one said with a sudden, cackling laugh. "I caught her. She's mine."

"Not unless you want a bullet in your long gut to go with her," Fargo said. He met the stare in the strange eyes when the movement erupted at his right, and he half whirled to see the other man diving at Abigail, a curved skinning knife in his hand. He slammed into her, landed half over her with the knife blade held to her throat. Abigail's eyes were round with terror as she lay with the blade resting against her larynx.

"Now what were you saying about a bullet, mister?" the tall one said, and Fargo met the mirthless smile with tight-lipped anger. "Your gun, trap robber. Throw it over in the bushes," the man said. "Nice and easy." Fargo glanced at Abigail's terror-stricken face, and the knife pressed against her throat. He swore silently as he lifted the Colt from its holster and threw it the few yards into the nearest bush. He saw the tall man draw a heavy hunting knife from the back of his belt, a glistening eight-inch blade with a horn handle. "Now, I'm going to show you what happens to trap-robbin' varmints," the man hissed. "Then I'll be enjoying the little lady at my leisure."

Fargo half circled as the long, thin figure came at him. The man's pale blue eyes were blazing with a wild light, a twisted smile on the long, cadaverous face. The man tried a quick slash of the blade, and Fargo instinctively ducked away, feeling the blade all but graze his shoulder. The man's gangly arms were a danger, their reach unexpectedly long.

Fargo backed as the man moved toward him again, the evil smile frozen on the long, sunken face. The man lunged, a sharp, sudden movement, and Fargo sidestepped easily, started to bring a blow up but held back as one long arm sent the knife in a backhanded slash.

He moved in a half crouch as the tall figure turned to face him again. The long, gangly form was not well coordinated, he saw, but he still had to twist away fast as the man lunged again and the blade grazed the top of his shoulder. Long legs and long arms made the figure dangerous, Fargo realized as he half circled to the left, then to the right, and drew two more long-legged lunges that missed by inches. The long face lost its smile, and a snarl twisted the lips as the tall form lunged again, tried to swerve midway, and sent the knife in a wide arc that missed its target. As the long figure awkwardly tried to spin, Fargo came in low and smashed a long, right hook into the man's midsection. The long figure doubled almost in two with a grunt of pain, and Fargo crossed a whistling left hook that caught the man on the point of the jaw. The long-legged form arched backward, long arms and legs flailing the air, and landed hard on its back.

Fargo stepped in quickly with a looping left hook that caught the man alongside the temple as he tried to pull his long legs up. The tall figure twisted half around and sprawled on the ground, but the man kept his hold on the long-bladed knife. He swiped out with it as Fargo tried to come in again, and the Trailsman had to leap backward as the slash just missed his legs.

The man seized the moment to collect his long body and get to his feet. He lunged with driving speed, long arms slashing the air. Fargo saw the blade coming at his chest. He stayed crouched a moment longer, ticked off split seconds, and dropped as the long blade whistled over his head. The tall figure slammed into his crouched body at the knees, and as the man hit, Fargo straightened up with all the power of his legs and shoulders lifting upward. The man catapulted into midair, long, gangly legs flailing outward. He slammed into the ground, and Fargo heard his gargled scream. The sound trailed off in a series of throaty gasps. Fargo rose, turned to see the bone handle of the knife protruding from the man's belly. The long figure drew its legs upward, straightened, twitched violently for a moment, and lay still.

Fargo stepped to the bushes, scooped up the Colt, and turned to the second man, who still lay half over Abigail, his skinning knife still against her throat. He glanced back at Fargo. "I'll kill her, goddamn, I will," the man threatened, and Fargo saw his hand holding the knife tremble, his oily face showing fear as well as desperation. Fargo kept his voice even, almost nonchalant.

"You do that and you're a dead man," he said. "Let her go and you walk out of here alive." The man's eyes stared back at him as he struggled to make a decision, plainly not a process he was used to handling. "You've my word on it," Fargo added.

The little eyes blinked. "Maybe your word's shit," the man threw back.

"Maybe," Fargo agreed, still keeping his tone calm. "That's a chance you'll have to take. You only know one thing for sure. Cut her and you're dead. Guaranteed." He saw the man lick his lips nervously, but he kept his own face coolly unconcerned. Inwardly he cursed; he knew that terror shriveled Abigail as she lay helpless. He had the Colt in position to fire, and he thought about risking a shot but decided against it. Even if his shot hit on target, the man's reflex action could send the knife across Abigail's throat. Instead he remained calmly motionless and watched the shine of perspiration appear across the other man's face. "I don't aim to wait all day," he said with quiet casualness.

"Your word, mister?" the man said.

"That's what I said," Fargo answered. The man waited a moment more, swallowed hard, and pushed himself up from Abigail in a quick motion. He stayed in a half crouch, his eyes on the big man with the Colt. Fargo let the Colt lower a half inch, and the man began to edge his way backward nervously. He made for the incline and erupted into a desperate burst of speed when he reached it. Fargo watched him race up the slope to the top and disappear down the other side before he holstered the Colt and reached Abigail in two long strides. She reached out to wrap both arms around him, and he felt her violent trembling. He held her tightly, and she made little sobbing noises, holding herself hard against him until the violent trembling finally subsided. She drew back finally, her direct brown eyes still filled with fear.

"God, I thought I was dead," she murmured. "I guess I would have been except for you."

"They were just a bad pair. Probably bad trappers too," Fargo said as he rose and pulled her to her feet. "Let's see if you can stand on that ankle," he said. She nodded but clung to him a moment longer, and he felt the soft pressure of her modest breasts against his chest before she pulled away.

"Thank you, Fargo," she said gravely. "That's not much for saving one's life, but it's all I have."

"Guess it'll have to do, then," he said, and stepped back and watched as she took a few tentative steps.

"It feels all right," she said.

"Leave it bandaged till tonight," he said, and Abigail walked to the brown mare with only a slight limp. "Let's ride," he said, and swung onto the Ovaro and led the way from the spruces. An apple tree provided breakfast, and a clear mountain stream offered them cool, refreshing water to drink and an opportunity to refill their canteens. He picked up the wagon tracks as they crossed over the next hill and began to move upward into the high mountain country. They followed a path between stands of balsam, mountain ash and silver maple. The terrain rose steadily, but the thick tree cover held little hills and dips in the land.

"You just follow the wagon tracks," he said to Abigail. "I'll be back."

"Where are you going?" she asked, instant alarm in her voice.

"Scouting," he said, and fastened her with a sharp glance. "You think you can follow orders now?" he asked.

Her eyes narrowed instantly. "That was unnecessary and in bad taste," she snapped.

"So's getting killed," he said, and sent the pinto up into one of the hills that flanked the path between the trees. He slowed as he moved through the tree cover of balsam, and his eyes scanned the ground as his mouth grew tighter. He rode on ahead, crossed to where the land leveled off for a hundred yards. There were more signs that tightened his jaw still further, and he halted to pick up part of a moccasin beside a tall rock. When he rode back down to the winding pathway below, he rejoined Abigail and knew that her eyes searched his face.

"You saw Indian signs," she ventured, and he nodded.

"Plenty of Sioux," he grunted.

"How do you know?" she asked, and he pulled the piece of moccasin from his pocket and tossed it to her.

"Quill work with beaded borders," he said. "Horizontal stripes across the top. Sioux. Most tribes have their own ways of decorating their moccasins." He increased the pace of the Ovaro, and Abigail speeded up to stay with him.

"What else is bothering you?" she asked.

"They're following but hanging back," he said. "That means they're usually waiting for the right moment to attack." Abigail lapsed into silence as he continued to set a fast pace until the sun had crossed into mid-afternoon. He halted at a small stream to let the horses drink, and Abigail took the bandage from around her ankle. She flexed her foot, and he knelt down beside her and ran his hands across the ankle, down over the back of her heel, and up to the lower calf. The swelling was all but gone, he noted.

"Feels all right," he said.

"You have a very gentle touch," she said.

"You're surprised." He laughed, and she shrugged. "Comes from checking out hundreds of pasterns and fetlocks," he said.

"You have a way of saying the right thing the

wrong way." She frowned with exasperation. "A woman hardly likes to be compared to a horse."

"Makes 'em feel inferior, probably," Fargo said, anticipating her hiss of breath. "Well, you have to expect that from those of us who appeal to women in a raw, animal way." He smiled and saw her face flood with pink.

"Sheila had no right to tell you that," she gasped.

"It was just a passing comment." He laughed again. "But you'd best be careful."

"Why?" She frowned.

He rose to his feet and pulled her up with him. "You never know when that raw, animal appeal might get to you," he said. She turned and strode to the brown mare, but the pink stayed in her cheeks, he saw. He laughed softly as he watched her swing the slender, narrow, graceful figure onto the horse.

He pulled the Ovaro ahead of her and led the way on, his eyes sweeping the land ahead as they rode. The day had drifted into dusk when he found a pond fed by a wellspring. "We'll camp here," he said. "You can take a dip before sleeping."

"I'd like that," she said. "So would you, I'm sure."

"You've a suspicious mind, Abigail," he said. "You've nothing to worry about."

"Are you saying you won't watch?" she asked.

His eyes went to the dusk sky and scanned the line of low clouds that crossed from north to south. Wearing a little smile at the edge of his lips, he said, "I'm saying there won't be a moon to see with," he said. "See those clouds? They're going to make it a black night. You can be as modest as if you were in your own bedroom."

"We'll see." Abigail sniffed, and he tossed her a

wide grin as he dismounted and unsaddled the Ovaro. The night came quickly and enveloped the land in almost total blackness. He sat down and chewed on the beef jerky out of his saddlebag, and Abigail was a dark shape beside him as she ate.

"It *is* black," she remarked. "I couldn't see you at all if I moved another two feet away."

"I told you that," Fargo remarked.

"Think the clouds will stay all night?" she asked.

"Long enough," he said. "You go in first."

"All right," Abigail agreed, and he saw her stand up and walk toward the edge of the pond with careful steps as she pushed her way through the blackness. She disappeared from his sight before she reached the pond, but he heard her shedding clothes as he lay back on the grass. The soft splashing sound drifted to him as she entered the pond, and he listened to her paddling in the water. He rested, arms behind his head, for another five minutes, then pushed himself up and started to pull his shirt off as he walked toward the pond. He put it on the grass at the edge of the water, dropped his gun belt atop it as he listened to Abigail moving about the little pond, the moonless blackness still cloaking her.

He looked up at the sky, waited, and saw the first pale white glimmer through the tail of a swift-moving cloud. Another cloud followed, shredded itself on the wind, and the pale white glow grew stronger. They had been scudding along fast, and he guessed they'd pass in a half hour. He'd been off by not more than five minutes. He grunted as the tail of the last cloud passed and the almost full moon spread its pale light down to bathe the little pond in soft brightness.

He turned at Abigail's sharp intake of breath, saw her standing in the water as she spied him and clasped her arms over her breasts. She sank down to her neck at once as he watched her.

"The moon," she gasped at him.

"Go to the head of the class," he said mildly.

"The clouds. They've gone," she said, her voice rising.

"That's two for you," he said.

"You said they'd last," she accused.

"Never trust a cloud," he commented.

"I know who never to trust. Damn you, Fargo," she snapped. He shrugged and drew off trousers and underwear and stepped into the pond. "What are you doing?" she exclaimed.

"Same thing you are," he said.

"You get out of here," she demanded.

"There's plenty of room for two. It's not that small a pond," he said as he dived, came up, blew water away. She hadn't moved, but she'd risen, her arms still crossed in front of her breasts. "You can leave," he said pleasantly.

"No," she threw back.

"Suit yourself," he said, and dived again. He swam underwater for a few feet and rose closer to her. She glared at him. He tossed her a smile and used a backstroke to swim away, turn, roll, and play in the cool water. When he surfaced after a dive, he was near the edge of the pond, and he felt the night wind growing sharp. He touched bottom and stepped out of the little pond, his wet body glowing in the moonlight that bathed the rippling muscles. He felt Abigail's presence in the water, suddenly a very desirable presence, and felt his flesh responding to his thoughts. He turned, sat down on the grass, letting the cool wind dry him. Abigail remained with her arms folded in front of her.

"I'm getting cold," she said.

"I imagine so," he said. She flung an angry glance at him, dipped down, and swam toward him. He saw the big towel lying at the edge of the pond. She reached one arm out, picked the towel up, and held it high as she hopped out of the pond. She moved with quick deftness as she wrapped herself in the towel, but not before he caught a glimpse of long, thin legs, a long waist, and one side of a pertly upturned breast. He lay back on the grass at the edge of the pond as the wind continued to dry him and watched Abigail, the towel wrapped snugly around her, step toward him.

She halted almost beside him and threw a quick glance down the length of his powerful, muscled body where his maleness again responded to her presence. "Damn you, Fargo," Abigail said breathlessly. "Why are you doing this?"

"Why not?" he returned. "I don't wait for tomorrows that might never come. Tomorrow could bring me a Sioux arrow in the gut."

"That's a convenient excuse for indulging yourself," she snapped.

"You want another reason?" he asked. "Because I like to. Because you want to."

"No," she bit out.

"Liar." He laughed.

She spun on her heel and strode away from him. He let the wind dry the last drops from his skin before he rose and pulled on trousers only. He carried his gun belt and shirt with him as he returned to the little campsite. Abigail, wrapped in her robe, sat on a blanket, but her eyes lifted, followed him to his bedroll. Her voice cut through the silence, filled with admission carried inside accusation. "What makes you so damn sure I want to?" she threw at him.

"Same way I'm sure when a peach is ripe," he answered. "Or when a wood lily's ready to open."

Her silence answered, and he shed trousers and slid into his bedroll. The almost full moon bathed the ground. The pale light was nonetheless strong enough to outline objects clearly, and Fargo had turned on his side when he heard her footsteps. He rolled onto his back to see Abigail standing over him, frowning down at him.

"Damn you," she bit out as she tore the robe from herself. Flinging it aside, she stood before him, a silvery, naked wraith, the modest breasts turned beautifully upward, legs a little thin but fitting the very slender, narrow figure, a flat belly, small hips, and a small, dark triangle. Abigail dropped to her knees with one sudden, almost angry motion as he pulled out of the bedroll, and her arms were encircling his neck, her lips on his.

"No," she murmured as he let his hand cup one pert, modest breast, his thumb brushing slowly across the tiny nipple. "No," she repeated as she pressed the breast harder into his palm. He moved her back, onto the bedroll, and enjoyed the pert, upturned line of her breasts, tiny nipple softly pink, the circle around it deeper in color but equally tiny. He put his mouth to the soft, firm flesh, caressed with his tongue, sucked softly, and Abigail's cry was a gasped call of protest and pleasure intertwined. His hand traced a line along the underside of the other breast, cupped it, caressed, massaged the little tip as it hardened, and he felt her long, thin legs move, lift, draw knees up.

"No, oh, no," she murmured again as his fingers moved down the long-waisted body, exploring, caressing, sliding across the flat little belly and pushing through the little dark mossy nap. "Ooooh," Abigail half moaned as he pressed down over the small, almost flat pubic mound. He saw her legs straighten, then draw up again, both held tightly together, moving as one. They fell sideways to the right, then the left, moving as one, held tightly together, and as she drew her knees up again, his hand pressed down beyond the tip of the pubic mound.

"No, no, oh . . . oh," Abigail cried out as she held her legs tightly together. He moved his hand back, and the legs flailed back and forth together and drew up again. She brought one hand up around his neck, pulled his face down harder onto one modest breast. "Ah, ah . . . ah," she gasped out as he caressed the upturned mound with his lips, his tongue flicking back and forth across the top of the tiny nipple as her hand dug into the back of his neck. Her hips were twisting, turning, but her legs stayed together. He shifted, brought himself half over her, and pressed the warm, throbbing, anxious shaft down over her.

Abigail screamed as though she'd been stabbed, but the protest in the cry trailed away to desire as little whimpered sounds followed. Her hands moved down to press into the small of his back as he lay half atop her. He pressed with his thigh, brought one leg onto her, moved it down. Abigail moaned as he pressed against her legs, pushed harder, got his leg between the tightly-held-together thighs, and let it rest there. Abigail quivered, her thin thighs pressed tight against his leg. He half rose, brought his eager organ down to press the tip against the very end of her little nap. Holding himself there, he listened to Abigail's gathering cry. He pressed, pressed harder, and suddenly the thin thighs fell away from his leg, and Abigail's pelvis pushed upward.

"Yes, oh, go on . . . oh, damn, oh, yes," she half screamed, and he felt her legs as they fell outward, came together, fell away again. He had only to shift his torso and the long, throbbing shaft slid into her, and her quick, gasped scream spiraled into the night.

He felt the tightness of her, but she was flowing around him, lubricating, welcoming, and he slid forward deeper. Abigail dug heels into the ground, drew back from him, and then almost leapt upward and forward in a tremendous thrusting motion that slammed all of her over the entire length of him. She screamed, dug heels in again, drew back, pulled breath in, and slammed her torso forward again as she screamed. He felt her heels dig into the earth again and again as she increased the speed and force of each thrusting collision of pelvis against pelvis, each time with a scream that tore from her.

She made love with a strange combination of wild passion and fury, a frantic desire that seemed to rise out of some racing inner turmoil. She cried out sharp sounds as he drew back and slammed forward to meet her every thrust, and, when he heard the sudden, quick gasps and felt her fingers digging into the small of his back, he let himself explode with her. Abigail screamed as she came, screamed again and again, and inside the ecstasy there still lay a core of angry protest. But he smiled as she sank limply down under him. The protest had fueled desire and heightened pleasure, enabling her to reach absolute heights of ecstasy. He kissed each modest breast gently as she lay still and let her breath return.

Her hands rose, pressed his face down onto one breast, and she held him there until her breath returned to normal. She then let him lift his face. She stared at him, a frown touching her brow, closed her eyes, and went to sleep at once, curled up against him, drawing knees up to lay half across his legs. He let sleep sweep over him with her.

He woke with the morning sun, saw that she had hardly moved, and enjoyed the slender loveliness of her for a long moment before he pulled himself out from under her. She only stirred, and he rose, washed, and dressed beside the pond and found her still asleep when he returned. He reached down and shook her, and she made little noises. He shook her harder and her eyes opened. A family trait, he started to say but thought better of it. "Time to move," he said, and Abigail blinked, nodded, and sat up, the twin, pert breasts pointing upward with a fresh, eager curve to them. He turned away and began to saddle the horses as she trudged to the pond with her clothes, still rubbing sleep from her eyes.

He had the horses saddled when she returned in the brown riding skirt and brown-checked shirt. A half glower held her face, and she peered at him as though she could find something for herself in his face. "It's too nice a morning for frowns," he commented as he swung onto the pinto.

"I don't understand myself," Abigail muttered as she went to the brown mare and shook her head, her curly brown hair bouncing from side to side. "I don't know what got into me," she said.

"You want to put that another way," Fargo remarked blandly, and saw the pink flush her cheeks.

"You know what I mean, dammit," Abigail snapped as she rode off beside him. "It just happened. I didn't want to, and yet I did."

"Because only part of you didn't want to," he told her. "Don't waste time thinking about why you did it."

"What would you suggest I think about?" Abigail frowned.

"When you're going to do it again," Fargo said as he sent the Ovaro into a fast canter. He picked up the wagon tracks that continued across the hills and set a fast pace as he saw the wagons had slowed, stopping often to rest as the slopes grew more steep. "We're making good time," Fargo told Abigail as she stayed close behind him. He pulled to a halt at a place where a runoff had soaked the earth. He dismounted, ran his fingers along the wheel grooves in the softened soil. The edges were firm, refusing to crumble at his touch. "They can't be very far ahead," he said to Abigail as he remounted, pausing for a moment to let his eyes sweep the surrounding terrain. He saw nothing to alarm him and sent the horse into a canter again.

A flat stretch opened up between a large stand of alders and a shrub-covered slope of rock formations, and he reined to a halt to frown at the wagon tracks. "They separated here," he muttered. "What the hell for?" he wondered aloud. One set of tracks turned up into the rock formations of the slope while the other set continued on straight across the flat land.

"What now?" Abigail asked.

"We follow this set," Fargo said as he sent the pinto up the slope of rock formations.

"Why this set?" Abigail questioned.

"They'll be going real slow up this slope. They'll be the easiest to catch up to," he told her, and his eyes swept the pinnacled rock formations that rose up on all sides. The path turned and twisted, the terrain made of tall rock formations, big, round boulders and jagged crags, all dotted with stands of lodgepole pine. It was land made for surprise attacks, harboring a hundred convenient hiding places, and he moved the pinto along carefully as his eyes scanned the rocks. Abigail stayed close behind him, and he felt the pinto struggle for footing as the trail rose and the ground became covered with small, loose pebbles. The wide-wheeled wagons would have an easier time of it than the horses. He grunted, then spotted the top of the trail only a dozen yards away as his nostrils suddenly flared. He halted, drew in the air again, and Abigail stopped beside him.

"I smell something burning," Abigail said, sniffing the air. Fargo felt the line of his jaw grow tight, and he held the oath inside himself as he drove the pinto sharply up the remainder of the upward trail. The oath refused to stay held in as he reached the top of the incline.

"Goddamn," he murmured as he stared at the small hollow of rock and the charred remains of four wagons. A wisp of smoke still curled up from the rear of one wagon, and his eyes swept the broken-doll figures that lay on the ground and draped over the burned remains of the wagons—men, women, children, barely recognizable as such. He saw three women to the side, naked, hung on a single lodgepole pine, their bodies torn, slashed, scalped. He could only imagine that they had welcomed death.

"Oh, my God," he heard Abigail's murmur. "I'm going to be sick." She had come up behind him, and now she turned the brown mare and slid from the saddle. He heard her throwing up as he moved the Ovaro closer to the charred wagons. The Sioux had used tomahawks to hack the wagons apart before setting fire to them, he saw. Most of the occupants had been hacked apart also. His hand flew to his side, and the big Colt was in his grip, ready to fire, as he heard a stone dislodge a dozen feet above him and roll noisily down the slope.

"Don't shoot. Jesus, don't shoot, mister," he heard a voice call.

"Get out where I can see you," Fargo said, and glimpsed Abigail stepping closer, her eyes on the rocks above. Fargo watched the figure move into view from behind a flat-topped tower of stone, graying, long hair, a battered hat, an old tan vest, and worn trousers. "Get down here," Fargo ordered, and the man scrambled down the rocks, landed almost at his feet, and pulled himself up. Fargo saw sharp blue eyes all but hidden in crinkled folds of skin, a parchment face with a grayish beard. He saw a short-handled pick hanging from the man's belt.

"Been hiding up there, afraid to come out," the man said.

"Since when?"

"Since early this morning," the man said. "Name's Jethroe Simms."

"How'd you get away?" Fargo questioned.

"I wasn't with the wagon train. I was coming down the mountain to visit with them when the damn red-skinned savages hit," Jethroe Simms said. "Must've been a dozen of them at least." He paused, blew air from between his lips, and used a red kerchief to wipe his forehead. "I left my mule and dived behind that rock when I saw them coming at the wagons. Damn mule ran off somewhere, and I guess I was lucky for that. If the redskins had seen him, they'd have come looking for me."

"You see the attack?" Fargo asked.

"Through a crack in the rock. Terrible, real bad," Jethroe Simms said, and his face darkened with disgust. "Sioux."

"You sure of that?" Fargo asked.

"Mister, I know Sioux when I see them. Been mining in these mountains all my life," Jethroe Simms snapped. "This bunch was led by a big one with a chest like a barrel of ale."

Fargo shot a glance at Abigail. "That's how Sheila described the Sioux that took Bobby," he said.

"Does that mean anything?" she asked.

"I don't know. But it means he's not far away," Fargo said, his lips tightening into a thin line. "Probably no farther than the other four wagons," he said.

"I didn't see any other four wagons," Jethroe Simms cut in.

"They separated from this group and stayed on a trail below," Fargo said, and wheeled the Ovaro around. "Let's get to them before it's too late."

"Wait, I'm not stayin' here alone, and God knows where that damnfool mule's got to," the old miner said. "I'll go with you. I'll ride one of the extra horses behind the last wagon. If you're going after those Sioux, I'll be happy to give you another gun."

"Get the horse," Fargo said, and waited as the miner secured one of the extra horses, a dark brown gelding, pulled himself on it, and hurried over to the incline that led down. "Name's Fargo, Skye Fargo. This is Abigail Snow," the Trailsman said. "We can talk more later."

He sent the Ovaro down the steep incline as fast as the horse could handle the loose rocks of the terrain. He reached the bottom where the wagon tracks had separated, glanced back to see Abigail and Jethroe Simms making their way down, and sent the pinto racing along the flat land, following the second set of tracks. He kept the pinto full out while the ground stayed flat. The wagon wheel marks were clear, and he slowed only when the ground rose, the trees crowded in, and the grass grew very thick.

Abigail and Jethroe caught up to him as he paused to study a place where the ground turned hilly again, and he saw the snapped branches where the wagons had turned and gone through the trees. He led the way forward and had gone perhaps another half mile when he heard the shots, scattered, interspersed with whooping war cries. He sent the pinto racing forward again and reined up where the trees thinned around a cleared stretch of land.

The four wagons had made a makeshift circle, and he saw the Sioux racing around them, firing arrows mostly, and an occasional rifle shot. In typical Sioux tactics they were staying well out of range, darting in to fire clusters of arrows and dart back again. The incessant circling and yelling were aimed at shredding nerves and wasting ammunition, he knew, and he swept the Sioux as they continued to race around the wagons. Jethroe had been right: There were about a dozen, and the four wagons were holding their own so far. That would end soon enough when the Sioux's darting attacks grew sharper, faster, and more concentrated.

Fargo glanced at Abigail and the old miner as they halted beside him. "You've a rifle," he said to Abigail. "You're going to use it." She nodded, and he pointed to the tree cover that circled to the right side of the cleared land. "You and Jethroe move halfway down there, but stay back in the trees. I'll circle around to the other side. When I start to fire, you start shooting, you with the rifle, Abigail. Try to get some of them, but don't worry if you don't. The important thing is to shoot and keep shooting. Pour lead at them. I'll be doing the same from the other side."

He saw Jethroe Simms nod his graying head. "They'll hightail it. For now, at least. It'll sound like there are a whole posse of us, and they won't risk staying out in the open," the man said, and Fargo nodded. He watched Jethroe and Abigail make their way inside the edge of the trees before pushing the Ovaro down along the other side. The Sioux had begun to tighten their attack, he saw, as they sent in double sets of darting raiders and showered the nearest wagon with arrows aimed high and low. Fargo found a spot in the trees, turned the horse, and drew the big Sharps from its saddle holster. His eyes swept the racing Sioux. On the far side, watching his braves, he glimpsed the Indian with the big barrel chest. The description had been accurate. The man was lean and long from the hips down, thick and powerful from the hips up. He was out of range, and Fargo drew a bead on a racing Sioux that came in front of him. He fired, and the Indian catapulted from his pony as though he'd been yanked off. Fargo fired again and heard Jethroe and Abigail begin to shoot with furious volleys. He let go another fusillade from the big Sharps, saw the Sioux break off their circling, and race to where the big, barrel-chested leader waved them back toward him.

Fargo continued to fire though they were out of range, and he saw the Sioux fall in line behind the big-chested one and race into the trees. He stopped firing and listened. The attackers continued to race away, the sounds of their ponies crashing through the brush and trees in the distance. Fargo holstered the big Sharps and rode slowly from the trees toward the four wagons. Jethroe and Abigail moved into the open from the other side. A half-dozen men stepped from behind the wagons as he reached them, and Jethroe drew up with Abigail. One man with a neatly trimmed white beard and a flat-brimmed hat came forward.

"Praise be to you, friends," he said gratefully. "Are there others?"

"I'm afraid not," Fargo said.

"Push those wagons open and let these good folks in," the man ordered. Fargo saw others appear, a half-dozen women, and one of the Conestogas was pulled aside to make an opening between the wagons. Fargo rode into the circle, Abigail and Jethroe with him, and his glance swept the young faces that peered with frightened eyes from the wagons. Fargo swung to the ground and turned to the man with the neat white beard. "I'm Robert Anderson, wagon master," the man said.

"I'm Fargo," the Trailsman said, his voice cold, and he saw the man's eyes widen in surprise.

"Saints be," Anderson murmured. "I left word for you in Ironwood that we had to go on. I figured the binder we sent you would pay you for your trouble."

"Only you didn't have to go on without me," Fargo said.

Robert Anderson stared at him. "We were told we did," he answered. "Truth is, I was having real misgivings."

"Where's the man you took on as trailsman? Name's Zeke Marston, I was told," Fargo asked.

Robert Anderson's face grew dark with a frown. "He was with us till last night. He rode off to look around some and never came back. When he didn't show this morning, we went on. I couldn't understand it. I'm wondering if the Sioux caught him."

"Why'd you split up?" Fargo asked.

"Zeke Marston said it'd be better if we did. He sent the other four wagons up a high rock slope yesterday. He told us two sets of four wagons would be less apt to attract Indians than a long line of eight," Anderson said.

"Shit," Fargo heard Jethroe mutter, and the Trailsman nodded agreement.

"Marston split you into two easy targets," Fargo said. "We found the other four wagons. You're the lucky ones so far."

"My God," the man muttered, and the others

echoed his groan. "Why?" he asked the big man. "Why?"

Fargo glanced at Abigail and saw the same question in her eyes. "I don't know," he said. "But you were sent out on purpose, frightened into going without me. You were sent out as sitting ducks, set up with a tracker who took you far enough and then ran out."

"We didn't do anything to anybody. There's no reason for this," someone said, and Fargo met Abigail's eyes.

"Sam Monroe," she murmured.

"Sure as hell looks like it," Fargo said.

"But why? Where's the sense of it? And where does it fit in with Bobby?" She frowned.

"Goddamned if I know." Fargo frowned back. "There's no rhyme or reason that I can see. Only there has to be." He saw Jethroe frowning at him. "I'll fill you in later," he said before turning his eyes back to the wagon master. "Turn your wagons around and get back to Ironwood. You can't make it with only four wagons, especially with the Sioux on the warpath," he said. "Go back and wait for another four wagons to join up. Then you can try again."

"The horses are real tired and so are we. It'll take us maybe five days to make Ironwood. They could attack us anytime along the way," Anderson said.

"They could, but five days is better than the two weeks or more it would take if you went on. Besides, if you're headed back, they might just let you go," Fargo said. "Try to go on and you're dead for sure, if not by the Sioux then by the Assiniboin or the Northern Cheyenne or maybe the Crow."

He waited as the man's shoulders slowly sagged,

and he turned to the others. Their grave, strained faces spoke without words. "We'll go back," the wagon master said.

"You've a good part of the day left. Start now," Fargo said, and he watched as the others turned away and began to clamber onto their wagons. It took only a few minutes for the Conestogas to begin to file away, and Fargo saw Robert Anderson wave back at him from the first wagon. He didn't return the wave. The man had been tricked, scared, and cajoled into going on without waiting. But he had used a fool's judgment, and Fargo had no use for fools.

"Maybe you'd like to fill me in some," he heard Jethroe Simms suggest, and he nodded as he lowered himself to the thick grass and stretched out his long frame. He told Jethroe about Bobby's capture, about Sheila and Sam Monroe, and about whatever else held any importance. When he finished, Jethroe peered at him with his lips pursed.

"Sure as hell is a strange one, all right," the man said. "It seems to point at this Sam Monroe feller, but it doesn't make any sense."

Fargo pulled his lips back in grim agreement. "You saw the Sioux attack. They stayed around some after they finished. You hear anything that might help?" Fargo asked. "You talk Sioux?"

"Some. Enough to horse-trade for my scalp if I have to," Jethroe said. "The chief is called Bear Chest, and he's mad as hell about something."

"Maybe he's just always mad as hell," Abigail put in.

"You want to try to find him?" Jethroe asked. "There's a Sioux camp over the other side of the first mountain range. About three miles from here,

I'd guess. I came on it by accident and got the hell away fast. But I marked the spot in my head so's I wouldn't make the same mistake twice."

Fargo saw the hope spring into Abigail's eyes. "Let's go take a look," he agreed.

"It better be a damn careful look," Jethroe grunted as he climbed onto his horse.

5

Jethroe led the way up a steady climb where lodgepole pine and tamarack provided most of the tree cover. "I appreciate this very much," Abigail said to the old miner as they rode. "Not many people would risk their necks for someone else."

"That story of yours has my curiosity up—but it's not just that," the old miner said. "That Sioux chief is bad medicine. I'd like to see him out of the way so things can calm down again and I can mine these mountains more or less in peace."

"You ever see him before the attack this morning?" Fargo asked.

"No, and I know some of the Sioux around here. I'd guess he came from down past Beaverhead Range," Jethroe said. "I'd heard that some of the hotheaded Sioux had come up this way."

The old miner was a storehouse of legend and lore amassed over a lifetime of living in these moutains, Fargo realized. "You ever hear of any reason for the

Sioux to take a little boy? Any special sacrifices or ceremonies?" he asked.

"None," Jethroe said. "This whole thing is sure one strange piece of business. You don't even have a reason why Sam Monroe sent that wagon train out here."

"No, I don't," Fargo admitted grimly as Jethroe slowed his horse when they reached the top of the climb. A broad ridge stretched out ahead of them, and Fargo watched the red ball of the sun disappear behind the high peaks. Purple dusk began to settle on the mountains, and Jethroe reined to a halt. He pointed to a trio of tamaracks some half mile distant, which formed a straight line.

"The Sioux camp is just past those three trees, down in a little hollow," Jethroe said.

"It's too early even to try to get close," Fargo said, and pulled the Ovaro into a clump of lodgepole pine to one side of the wide ridge. "We'll have to wait at least an hour before I can try," he said as he swung from the saddle.

"I'll be back in an hour," Jethroe said.

"Where are you going?" Fargo frowned.

"Halfway down the way we came. This is country that old mule of mine knows and likes. He just might have headed back here. I can look around while you're waiting. Hell, all my gear's on that mule," Jethroe said.

"I'll be here," Fargo said, and Jethroe turned his horse and disappeared over the edge of the ridge. Fargo sat down, made himself comfortable, and Abigail came to kneel beside him.

"Hold me," she said softly. "I'm very afraid." She waited, little-girl-like, until he took her in his arms. She came against him, one hand finding its

107

way inside his shirt. She lay quietly, and suddenly he felt her fingers unbuttoning his shirt, her hand sliding across his powerful pectoral muscles. "I want to be closer," she said, and pressed against him. He felt her fingers moving again, this time unbuttoning her own shirt. "I want to be more close," she whispered as she pressed the softly firm, pert breasts against him.

His hands grasped the waistband of her skirt, flipped open buttons, and slid the garment from her. His hand clasped around her tight, narrow little rear, pressed, and she wriggled and gasped. Her hands pulled at his gun belt, opened buckles, undid trousers, and he drew his legs up as she slid his clothes off. She gasped as her hand brushed against his organ, which had already begun to rise, thicken, throb. She drew away, then returned her hand, and curled her fingers around him.

"Oh, Fargo . . . oh, oh, my," Abigail said breathlessly. She held him, pulled him to her flat little belly, and pressed him against her. Then she turned, lifted her hips, and pulled his toward her with feverish haste. "Quick, oh, quick, before he comes back. Before I can think about tomorrow. Oh, please, please," Abigail gasped out. He turned, came to her, and slid inside her. He felt her pelvis lift, draw back as once again she dug her heels into the ground and slammed herself forward in violent, thrusting pleasure.

Again she surprised him by her intensity, the quivering, furious thrustings each time she rammed herself onto the full length of his shaft. Almost as though she wanted punishment with her pleasure, she drew back, rammed forward, and half screamed each time until he felt her begin to tremble. He drew back, almost to the tip of her portal, and rammed forward to match her wild thrust as she exploded. Her thin legs pressing against him, her arms encircling his neck, she quivered against him as she made tiny gasping sounds.

Finally she fell away and lay beneath him, her direct brown eyes staring up at him. "You didn't have to hurry that much," he said. "I don't think Jethroe will be back for another half hour." She didn't answer, and he smiled. "But it wasn't because of Jethroe, was it?" he said.

"It takes over. I become afraid it won't happen. I feel I have to make it happen quickly," Abigail admitted.

"And punish yourself for letting it happen," he said. "Next time slow. Slow and easy. Only pleasure."

"All right." She nodded. He rose, began to dress, and she quickly pulled on clothes with him. Her eyes were grave and unsmiling when she faced him. "Will there be a next time?" she asked.

"I sure as hell hope so," he said, and turned as he heard the sound of a horse moving up the slope. Jethroe came into view alone, and Fargo glanced at the moon. It was time to move, and he swung onto the Ovara as Abigail followed. Jethroe brought up the rear as he rode forward across the wide ridge until the three tamaracks were clearly outlined under the moon. "This is as far as you two go," he said as he reined to a halt.

"This is plenty far enough for me," Jethroe said, but Fargo saw the protest forming in Abigail's eyes.

"If I'm going to find out anything I've got to get close enough to see their camp," Fargo said. "The only way I'll make it is alone." She nodded reluctantly, and he put his hat over the saddle horn and handed her the reins.

"How long do we wait?" Jethroe asked. "You could get yourself pinned down someplace."

"I know." Fargo nodded. "Wait till dawn. If I'm not back by then, hightail it out of here."

"Good enough," Jethroe said, and Fargo slowly walked on, the three tall tamaracks almost directly in front of him. He passed the trees and started down the other side of the slope. He was surrounded by thick mountain brush, pines, and plenty of rock as he carefully made his way down, testing each step before he took it. He'd gone halfway down the slope when he smelled the scent of wood burning and the smell of meat hanging on drying racks. He heard the sounds as he moved down father; murmured voices and the soft glow of the campfire began to filter into the darkness.

He grew grateful for the rocks that lined the way down as he stayed behind them, making quick, darting moves from one to another until he could see the encampment. He halted, slid around a tall, smooth boulder, and dropped to his knees behind a line of heavy mountain brush. It afforded him a view of the entire camp. He took in four tepees first, one larger than the others and set back from the rest. He slowly scanned the camp. There was one meat-drying rack, a few old squaws moving about, and a single fire in the center of the clearing. No permanent base camp here. He grunted silently. A field camp set up for quick disbanding. A half dozen bucks sat near the fire, and he saw two more leave the nearest tepee. He shifted his glance to the largest of the tepees and saw three braves standing guard outside it. As he watched, the flap of the tepee opened and the figure stepped outside. The man's huge, barrel chest was unmistakable.

The Sioux's black eyes scanned the camp out of a broad, flat face. Fargo took in the power of the huge chest and the thick arms that tapered down to the thin torso and legs that didn't seem to belong on the same body. The Indian stepped forward, grunted commands, and one of the braves brought him a piece of meat from the fire. He tasted it and sent it back with a grunt of disapproval, and Fargo saw the row of buffalo ribs on the fire he hadn't noted before. They were expecting company, he guessed, and he kept his eyes on the bear-chested Sioux as the man turned to another of the tepees and raised his voice in a barked command. The flap of the tepee pulled open, and an old, toothless squaw came out with a young girl, perhaps ten years old, Fargo guessed.

The girl, dressed in a beaded elk skirt, wore a necklace with a single bear's claw on it. Two little, barely formed breasts were tentative, coppery mounds on her chest. She halted beside the Sioux chieftan, and he ran his hand across the black hair that already hung beneath her young shoulders. The girl and he spoke almost in whispered tones, but Fargo caught the word *daughter* repeated twice. The Sioux was plainly proud and fond of the young girl. Before she left to return to the tepee, he took her face in his hands for a moment, and Fargo heard him say "daughter" again. The word was unmistakable in the Sioux tongue.

The young girl retired into the tepee under the watchful eye of the old crone, and Bear Chest seated himself cross-legged before the fire. He sat almost motionless, and time seemed to stand still until

Fargo picked up the sound of horses moving toward the camp from the other side. He saw the braves spring to their feet, bows and tomahawks in hand, as they lined the perimeter of the tepees. Peering across the fire, Fargo saw the horsemen slowly ride into the camp and form a half circle at the other side of the fire. He counted ten Sioux braves on their ponies.

Bear Chest rose as the visitors dismounted and exchanged greetings with a tall, hawk-nosed brave who appeared to be the spokesman for the others. He gestured to the meat on the fire, and the new-comers sat down and began to take of the meat, using long, pointed sticks to pull each piece to them. The meal was obviously a welcome, and Fargo strained his ears to catch enough words to make it plain that the visitors had arrived to join with Bear Chest's forces. But the Sioux chief had his back to him and spoke in deep, low tones. Fargo moved from behind the tall brush, slipped behind a boulder, and staying low, risked moving still closer to where a line of uneven rocks bordered the very edge of the campsite. He crouched, peered between the rocks, and could feel the heat of the fire as a soft wind blew toward him. He could hear Bear Chest easily now, and as he watched the meal come to an end, Bear Chest lifted one hand and gestured toward his tepee.

One of the three guards lifted the flap of the tent, and as Fargo watched, two braves emerged at once, a young boy held between them. Fargo saw dark brown eyes, a short, upturned nose, brown hair, and a face that echoed Sheila's. The boy was still clothed in his shirt and knickers, Fargo noted, and his young face tried unsuccessfully not to show fear.

Bear Chest gestured to the boy, and the two braves yanked Bobby up straight as the other Indians looked at him with expressionless stares. The Sioux chief waved his hand, and the two braves pulled Bobby back into the tepee.

Bear Chest began to talk to his new braves excitedly, gesturing with both hands. His voice reached Fargo clearly now. As Fargo listened he felt the frown dug into his forehead becoming a deep furrow. He knew the Sioux tongue well enough to catch most of what the Sioux chief said, and the few phrases he missed didn't change the heart of what he heard. He felt the disbelief that had first flooded over him at the Indian's words turn to a churning knot of cold anger as Bear Chest came to the end of his story.

The other Indians began to talk, but Fargo only half listened. He had heard more than enough when Bear Chest told about his capture of Bobby. No ordinary coup, this—no raid to mark down at the council fires just to show skill and daring. Fargo's eyes went to the chief's tepee, his glance moving across the three guards outside. There were at least two more inside, he knew, and he cursed silently. Too many, too damn many to give him a chance of even reaching Bobby, to say nothing of getting the boy out.

He had to find another way. Fargo frowned, and his eyes swept the camp again. But he saw nothing that triggered thoughts. Bear Chest's deep voice drifted to him as the Indian spoke of attacking the white men. Fargo swept the tepee again with a probing glance. Bobby was being kept under guard. How long he'd stay that way depended on Bear Chest's moods and whims. But the Sioux planned to roam and raid again. That meant that he'd take most of his warriors with him, leaving only the guards to watch his captive.

Maybe that was the chance to get Bobby, Fargo pondered: a sudden surprise attack when Bear Chest and most of his braves were scouring the mountains for more wagon trains. That meant holing up with Jethroe and Abigail and waiting for Bear Chest to ride out. Fargo's face crinkled up. The waiting didn't set well with him. It left too much in the Sioux's hands. Yet there seemed no other way with even a chance at succeeding, he conceded unhappily as his eyes probed the camp again. The tepee with Bobby inside it was just too heavily guarded.

Fargo had just decided to return to Abigail and Jethroe when two of the braves jumped to their feet and barked alarms. Fargo stayed in place as he saw them scan the perimeter of darkness around the camp. Others got to their feet and lifted their heads high as they sniffed the air. With a sinking feeling in the pit of his stomach, Fargo realized what had happened, and he cursed silently. They had suddenly smelled leather and wool and perspiration, white man's odors. The fire, he swore, the damn fire. It had warmed his clothes enough to bring out the scent of him. The Indians had picked it up at once. He cursed silently again.

Bear Chest had gotten to his feet and was sniffing the air as he peered into the dark beyond the edge of the camp. Fargo saw some of the others begin to spread out as they drew in odors. They hadn't zeroed in on him yet, but it was only a matter of time. They'd been set off, and they'd start searching. Surprise and maybe thirty added seconds was all he could get out of it now. He unholstered the Colt, drew a bead on one of the nearest braves, and fired. The Sioux spun as he went down, and Fargo saw the others drop down, some dive for cover, all reacting automatically.

He turned and began to race up the rocky slope. Perhaps he'd brought himself a whole minute. He grimaced as he glanced back. A few braves were starting to climb after him, but most were racing for their ponies. Fargo fired another shot, and the two starting to climb after him slid back and dropped behind a rock. He saw others on their ponies sweeping out of the camp at the other side of the fire. They were racing for what plainly was a passage that led up to the ridge. Fargo scrambled up, using brush to pull himself. The climb took only a minute or two, but it seemed forever till he reached the top of the slope. Abigail and Jethroe had heard the shots, of course, and he saw them peering toward him as he ran toward them along the top of the wide ridge. Abigail saw him first and started toward him, but he waved her back.

"Hit the saddle," he shouted, and she halted, backed to the brown mare, and mounted. He saw Jethroe pull himself onto his horse. Fargo made for the Ovaro, vaulted into the saddle, and wheeled the horse around. "No time to talk now. They'll be here any minute," Fargo said. "You two hightail it while I keep them busy chasing me. Right now they don't know you exist, and I want to keep it that way."

"Where do we wait for you?" Abigail asked.

"You don't. Go back to Ironwood. I'll meet you there," Fargo said.

"What about Bobby?" Abigail said.

"I saw him. Now get the hell out of here," Fargo bit out. Jethroe put his horse into a gallop, Abigail followed, and Fargo watched them ride along the wide ridge until the night swallowed them in its blackness. He turned in the saddle as he heard the sound of flying hooves pounding the ground and saw the Sioux appear from the other side of the ridge. He counted eight—Bear Chest not one of them—and sent the Ovaro full-out as he raced along the ridge the way Abigail and Jethroe had fled. But instead of cutting off and down the left side of the slope, he veered right to where the ridge dipped a dozen yards, and then rose up again to steep slope.

He heard the Sioux shouts and knew they'd seen him, and he raced the pinto down and then up the slope that led higher into the mountain range. He threaded through aspen and lodgepole pine and glanced back to see the Sioux split up. Four raced on along the bottom of the slope to cut him off if he tried to come down, while four started up the slope after him. As he watched, he saw those four split into two sets of two each, one pair moving to the right, the other to the left. They intended to out-flank him and perhaps force him to head down to where the other four were waiting, Fargo figured, his eyes narrowed. He shifted the Ovaro's direction to cut in front of the two moving up on the left and sent the horse into a deep cluster of pines. He pulled his lariat free, looped one end of it around the lowest branch of a young pine and backed the Ovaro into the trees. The rope lay loose on the ground, the other end in his hand, as he halted the Ovaro. His eyes watching the dark shapes of the two Sioux as they rode hard up the slope.

He coughed, saw the braves veer toward the sound at once and spur their ponies on faster. In the daylight they might have spotted the rope on the ground. In the dim moonlight they saw only the cluster of trees where their quarry had gone. Fargo waited, let them race into the pines, and almost cross in front of him before he yanked the lariat up and sent the Ovaro rearing backward. The rope snapped up, becoming steel-wire taut, and both Sioux slammed into it at neck level. They swept back off their ponies and hit the ground on their backs. They lay still. Fargo pushed forward, halted, and looked down at the two still forms, the mark of the rope a deep red line across their throats.

He turned and peered through the trees to see the other two circling back from where they had climbed. It would be easy enough to pick them off, but shots would bring the others from below. Instead Fargo let the Ovaro push noisily through a line of thick brush, and the two Sioux turned to follow instantly. Fargo continued on through the brush, slowed the Ovaro, and slipped from the saddle. He gave the horse a sharp pat on the rump, and the Ovaro moved a dozen steps more into the trees. Fargo crouched, drew the thin, double-edge throwing knife from the calf holster around his leg. He stayed crouched down as the second pair of searchers neared.

Glimpsing the tomahawks they gripped as they rode side-by-side through the brush he remained down. He watched them slow their ponies to a walk as they peered ahead. They came abreast of where he crouched, and Fargo drew the double-edge throwing knife back and waited, muscles tensed. It had to be quick and quiet with split-second timing, and he let another second go by. He let the Sioux nearest pass halfway by and the one beside him come into view. Then Fargo's arm came forward with all the strength of his powerful muscles, and the blade whistled through the night. But not at the nearest Sioux. Fargo had aimed at the one on the other side, and he heard the Indian's choking gasp as the knife hurtled into the side of his neck, imbedding itself to the hilt.

The Indian grabbed at his throat as it gushed red, but Fargo's eyes were on the other buck. As the Sioux turned to stare at his companion his back was to Fargo, and the Trailsman leapt forward and up, one long arm wrapping around the Sioux's neck. He yanked the Indian from the horse, fell back onto the grass with him, and before the Sioux could recover from his surprise, brought the butt of the Colt onto his forehead. The Indian's skin split, and a cascade of red began to run down across his face. Fargo pushed the Sioux away and stepped back. He glanced at the other one. The Indian lay on the ground, the throwing knife imbedded in the side of his neck, gave a last quivering motion, and lay still as blood continued to pour out of his mouth. Fargo pulled his knife free, cleaned it on the moist grass, and put it back into its holster.

He walked back to the Ovaro, swung up onto the horse, and moved from the cluster of trees. He peered down the slope and saw a rider moving upward, shifted his gaze, and saw another. The other four Sioux had put space between themselves and started to climb the slope. Fargo cursed softly. He'd been lucky so far. Everything had gone his way. He decided against pushing luck, and he turned the Ovaro and slowly began to walk the horse up the slope. He'd pulled up a few dozen yards when he set the horse into a canter and continued on up into the high land. The rocky, pine-strewn slope leveled off, grew steep again, offered a narrow ledge that let him ride across its rugged terrain.

He kept on and saw the first pink-gray streak of dawn edging the high peaks. Finding a high ledge he pulled to a halt. His eyes swept the slope below. Nothing moved nearby. The Sioux had broken off the pursuit or perhaps found the ones he'd done in and halted the chase there. Fargo watched the new day come in to sweep the mountains with bright sunlight. His gaze slowly scanned the slope below again. Satisfied that the Sioux had turned back, he dismounted and felt the tiredness of a sleepless night pull at him.

He slept in the hollow of a rock, and the night passed into a new day. He woke to the warmth of the sun. Staying in the high land, he made a wide circle before heading down. The maneuver kept him clear of Sioux search parties but took up most of the day. When he came down into the lower range, he knew he had lost a full-day's time. But he continued to ride carefully, keeping in tree cover wherever possible. A grim resolution rode with him, and he realized one stark fact: He had answers but no solution.

He rode at a steady pace, reaching the bottom of the lower range by dark. He found a ledge that afforded safety and comfort for the night and bedded down. He slept soundly and was in the saddle soon after the morning sun dawned. He continued to ride at a steady pace and estimated that he'd make Ironwood before nightfall. Abigail and

Jethroe would have reached the town at least a full day ahead of him if they hadn't run into trouble, and Abigail would tell Sheila that he had seen Bobby. It wouldn't make any difference, Fargo pondered. Sam Monroe could only give lip service to hope and wrestle with his own dark secrets.

The day began to wind itself down as Fargo reached the foothills where aspen and birch grew thick on hills that rolled gently instead of climbing into craggy peaks. But the night wrapped its dark arms around the land while he was still in the hills. The moon rose quickly as he continued on under its pale silver light. There was but one direct road into Ironwood, and Fargo cut across the hills that would lead him to it. He passed between two stands of birch, skirted a boulder that rose to his right, and sent the Ovaro up a slope that brought him on top of a low rise. He crested the ride, and the moonlight outlined horse and rider with silver clarity. The sound of the shot came to him at almost the same instant that the world became a blinding yellow flash. His temple seemed on fire.

He felt himself topple from the horse, fighting off the waves of unconsciousness that swept over him long enough to feel himself rolling. His head pounded, pained with an obliterating fury that swallowed up the world. He didn't know he rolled into rocks, hit against trees, slid off, and continued to roll until finally he lay still. His desperate effort to cling to consciousness had failed him halfway down the steep slope, and he lay unseeing, unhearing, unfeeling. The timeless void engulfed him, allowing only nothingness. Slowly the senses returned grudgingly. Feeling was a dull sensation, hearing a pounding in his ears, seeing a blurred grayness.

The dull sensation became touch, cold, roughness, smoothness. The blurred grayness shredded, formed shapes and objects, and the pounding in his ears finally ceased. He blinked, moved his head, and saw that he was lying on his side in a gulley way below the top of the rise. Slowly he pushed himself to a sitting position, wincing with pain as his head throbbed. He touched his temple and felt the caked blood there. The shot had struck a grazing blow, hard enough to do more than enough damage. A fraction closer and it would have killed him for certain. He touched the side of his head again and felt the caked blood all the way down to his jaw and neck.

He caught a faint silver glimmer at the bottom of the gulley and saw a little stream of water trickling its way through. He took his kerchief and slowly began to clean the caked blood from his face and temple. Every touch brought a grimace of pain to his lips, but he kept at his task until he had most of the caked blood cleaned away. He leaned back on his elbows to rest and took the time to curse at himself. He should have been more careful, he thought angrily. He'd grown careless and sloppy, letting himself become a clear target atop the rise. But most important, he had forgotten the cleverness of the desperate, and it had damn near cost him his life.

The moon was almost across the sky, he saw. It would be dawn in an hour. He had lain unconscious for most of the night. His gaze moved up the steep side of the gulley from where he'd fallen and he noted the marks where he'd rolled down. He pushed himself to his feet, swayed, fighting off a wave of dizziness, and cleared his head as he began to use pieces of brush to pull himself up the steep sides. He was climbing steadily, though painfully, when he spotted another set of marks alongside the ones he had made rolling down the gulley. They were heel marks dug deep into the ground.

His attacker had climbed down the side of the gulley but only halfway down, Fargo saw as the deep heel marks halted. His attacker had halted there and seen the blood streaming down the side of his victim's face from the temple. Satisfied that his shot had done its work he had pulled himself back to the top of the rise.

Fargo gritted his teeth and continued to pull himself up until he reached the top of the rise. He lay there a moment letting waves of pain and dizziness come and pass. Finally he rose and straightened. Hearing the sound first he saw the black-and-white shape trotting toward him. He leaned against the powerful neck for a moment before pulling himself into the saddle. He sat up straight, inhaled deeply, and moved the Ovaro slowly along the rise. He squinted down and picked up the marks where the rifleman had returned to his horse and headed down the other side of the hill.

Fargo moved the pinto after the hoofprints as he continued to take deep breaths. He rode slowly until he felt his body begin to revive. He quickened his pace then, and the dawn arrived, thin streaks of pink that slowly spread and turned the sky red. He followed the tracks that led south and away from Ironwood. The man had ridden slowly, walking his horse a good part of the time, Fargo noted. But he still had a six-hour start, and Fargo kept up a steady pace that devoured time and distance. He found where the man had bedded down for the night, paused to examine the ground, and saw that he had continued on south.

Fargo followed the hoofprints with dogged persistence through heavy ground growth that would have stopped most trackers. He lost the trail, picked it up again, had it disappear on him again, only to find it once more, relying on that special combination of sensitivity, ability, experience, and intuition that made him what he was, the Trailsman.

The sun had dipped to the horizon line when he glimpsed the lone rider ahead, moving through a line of hackberry. The man rode casually, confident that he was safe and secure, and Fargo swung the Ovaro directly behind the distant rider. He threaded his way through the trees, a silent shadow, as he drew closer to the rider in front of him. The land dipped, became a long, shallow hollow, and Fargo stayed at the high land along the edge of the hollow until he was abreast of the rider below. He pulled the Ovaro on and suddenly turned the horse and cantered down into the hollow and came into the clear a dozen feet ahead of the other man.

Fargo reined up, one hand resting on the butt of the big Colt at his hip. He saw the man's eyes stare at him, flick to the Ovaro, and return to him. "You ought never to take things for granted," Fargo said softly. The man continued to stare at him open-mouthed. Fargo saw a face with a dark stubble on it, dark eyes, and a flat nose. "Get off the horse," Fargo ordered. "Nice and easy. No fool moves. You're going to fill in a few details for me." The man brought his right leg up over the saddle and started to slide from the horse. As his feet touched the ground his hand flew to his hip. But Fargo saw the movement and fired from the saddle, a single shot that tore into the man's chest.

A cough came from the figure that suddenly had a hole where his chest had been, and a torrent of red spilled out of it. The man staggered backward two steps and slowly crumpled down into a grotesque sitting position that made him look like a Chinese Buddha that had been smashed down from the top. Fargo swung from the horse, took a step toward the figure as it slowly toppled on its side, a broken, lifeless shape.

"Damn fool," Fargo hissed through his teeth. He bent over the man and dug into his pockets. The right-hand pocket of his worn jeans offered nothing, but when Fargo drew his hand from the left pocket, he clutched a roll of bills inside a paper wrapper. A name was penciled on the wrapper around the bills, and Fargo let the name drop from his lips with bitter certainty before he read the wrapper. "Zeke Marston," he murmured, and glanced at the name penciled on the wrapper. It was only a confirmation, and he dropped the money onto the lifeless form where it quickly became what in actuality it was—blood money.

He turned away and pulled himself onto the Ovaro as the sun dropped below the horizon and night flooded the hills. He thought about bedding down and reaching Ironwood come morning, but he discarded the idea. If he pushed the Ovaro, he could make town before the night was too deep, and he seethed with an anger and a cold rage he wanted to spill out. But once again, as he turned everything that had happened in his mind—all of the dark, brooding secrets of greed and betrayal he had learned of—he realized that finding a solution might prove impossible.

He sent the pinto across the hills, retraced steps, and watched the moon as it moved slowly across the sky above him. When the Monroe house outside of Ironwood finally came into sight, he slowed the pinto to a walk. The moon was still an hour or so away from the midnight sky, he noted, and there were lights on inside the house. He rode silently to the front door, swung down from the saddle, and dropped the pinto's reins over the porch rail. He stepped to the door with one hand resting on the butt of the big Colt at his hip. He'd make no more mistakes, take nothing more for granted.

He knocked and heard footsteps approach on the other side of the door. When the door open, he looked into Sam Monroe's heavy face. He watched as the man's frown came first, then his jaw dropped, astonishment flooding the coarse, lined face.

"Surprise," Fargo said softly. Sam Monroe ran his tongue over lips suddenly dry. "If I didn't know better, I'd say you never expected to see me again," Fargo remarked bluntly. "But then you'd have no cause to think that, would you?"

"Didn't expect you at this hour," Sam Monroe managed to reply.

"It's not exactly a social call," Fargo answered.

Sam Monroe moved backward as Fargo pushed himself into the house. Abigail, wearing a long flannel nightgown, entered from an adjoining room. Her eyes became round saucers when she saw him, and she called out as she bolted past Sam Monroe and flung herself at Fargo's chest.

"*Sheila!*" she cried out as her arms encircled the big man. "Oh, God, we thought they'd caught you. Jethroe figured you should have reached here by yesterday," Abigail said as she leaned against him.

"Had a few delays," Fargo said with his eyes on Sam Monroe. Sheila ran into the room then, and Abigail stepped back as her sister raced to Fargo, her eyes dark and brimming with questions of hope and fear.

"Bobby, you saw Bobby! Was he all right?" she asked.

"He seemed so." Fargo nodded, anticipating her next question. "There was no way to get to him," he told her. "He's under heavy guard. Bear Chest still figures Bobby will bring him what he wants."

Sheila's eyes questioned, but Fargo saw Abigail frown. "What does he want?" she asked.

Fargo's glance went to Sam Monroe. "You want to answer that?" he asked almost casually.

"Why me?" the man blustered.

"Because you know what the Sioux want," Fargo answered, his voice still quiet.

"You're crazy, Fargo," the man snapped.

"You know what Bear Chest wants," Fargo said softly, and suddenly his voice was as cold as steel. "And you goddamn well know why he took Bobby."

Sam Monroe licked his lips again. "I don't know a damn thing," he said, but fear flickered his hard, gray eyes. Fargo heard Abigail's voice cut in, and his eyes went to her.

"What's going on? What are you saying, Fargo?" she asked.

"It seems that Sam has been trading rifles and ammunition to the Sioux for their best fur pelts," Fargo told her. "All very secret, of course. Only he sold the Sioux a batch of rifles that were no good. Bear Chest attacked an army patrol and lost fifteen of his best braves. That made him real mad."

"That's why he took Bobby? To get back at Sam?" Abigail frowned. "Revenge?"

"Revenge the Sioux way. He figured Sam Monroe would come chasing him to get his son back, and he'd fill him with Sioux arrows," Fargo said, turning his eyes to the man. "But that's where he made his mistake. He thought you cared about the boy. He didn't know you didn't give a damn about Bobby."

"You bastard. You rotten stinking bastard," Fargo heard Sheila's voice cut through the air. Her figure flew past him, arms outstretched as she tried to rake her nails across Sam Monroe's face. The man ducked away from her, and Fargo wrapped his arms around her waist and half spun, half lifted her away.

"That's not going to help anything now," he told her as he set her down and Abigail came to her side.

"You goddamn crazy woman," Sam Monroe shouted. "He's made all that up just to have somethin' to tell you for the money you paid him."

Fargo's eyes were blue spears of contempt as they bored into the man. "That's why you sent that wagon train out there, scared them into going on without me, even supplied them with a Trojan horse tracker. You sent them out there to be killed as an offering to the Sioux. That was the connection I couldn't make fit until I heard Bear Chest talk about it. You hoped that if he wiped out a wagon train, he'd be satisfied and back off."

"My God," Fargo heard Abigail whisper.

"Only it didn't work," Fargo said. "Bear Chest's still holding Bobby, still waiting for you to go after the boy."

"That explains those bushwhackers," Abigail said, awe in her voice. "He hired them to make sure I didn't convince you to look for Bobby. He was afraid finding Bobby might bring out the truth."

"Meanwhile Bear Chest is taking more braves on the warpath to kill as many settlers as he can," Fargo said grimly.

"What happens to Bobby when he gets tired of waiting for Sam to come rescue him?" Abigail questioned.

Fargo's face stayed harsh. There was no point in protecting Sheila from the truth any longer. "Bear Chest will kill him in frustration or sell him off to some other tribe in contempt," he answered.

"My God, my God," Sheila wailed, arms clasped around her breasts. "We've got to save him. We've got to go back there."

"That'll take some thinking," Fargo said. "The wrong move—a mistake, an attack that fails—and Bobby is a dead boy. You don't want to go rushing into this."

"A posse, one big enough that it can't fail," Sheila suggested.

"A real big one is sure to fail," Fargo answered. "Let me think of it. Bobby's still safe. Bear Chest is still waiting for the rooster to come after the chick." He turned to Sam Monroe and speared the man with ice-floe eyes. "Meanwhile you start drawing up a paper giving the store and everything in it to Sheila," he said.

"You're out of your goddamn head, Fargo," Sam Monroe yelled.

"You're going to be leaving town, anyway, soon as folks hear about your trading rifles to the Sioux," Fargo said. "Or swing from a rope."

"You've no proof. I'm important to this town. You haven't got a goddamn bit of proof, no evidence, nobody's word to back you up," Monroe threw at him.

"That's true enough. You saw to that," Fargo admitted. "Poor Ed Whiddle must have learned the truth. That's why he quit and began to drink himself into a stupor every day so he wouldn't have to face his conscience. But I'm not worried about proof. I've some settling up to do with you myself. I'll just include everybody else in."

"I don't take threats, Fargo," Monroe snarled.

"Good, because I don't take being shot by hired bushwhackers," Fargo returned, and brought his eyes to Sheila. Sam Monroe was a dangerous man, he knew. Monroe had replaced denial with callous, bullying confidence, and it was only part bluster, Fargo knew. He'd have to walk with one eye behind him now, ride with caution as his constant saddle mate. Sam Monroe had nothing left now but desperation. "Where's Jethroe?" Fargo asked Sheila.

"In town. Dolly's place, most likely. He said he'd give himself another day to wait for you. But that was yesterday," she said.

"I'll go find him. You get some sleep, and we'll talk more tomorrow," Fargo said. She nodded, and he caught Abigail's glance of gratitude as she walked from the room with Sheila. Fargo turned and locked eyes with Sam Monroe. "You're a miserable, lying, greedy, stinkin' bastard," he said almost with detachment. "You condemned I don't know how many innocent people to death because you tried to trick the Sioux. I aim to make sure you pay for it."

Sam Monroe swallowed, but his gray eyes stayed gimlet-hard. "Go to hell," the man cursed, and Fargo heard the door slam shut behind him as he walked from the house.

He rode into town and drew up at the saloon. When he strode in, he saw Dolly spot him at once, her fleshy face growing dour instantly. "Relax, honey. Came for a drink," he said.

"It's about time," Dolly grumbled as he let his eyes sweep the long bar. He found Jethroe at the far end, staring into a glass of beer.

"Bourbon," he said to the bartender as he stepped to the bar. Jethroe's head lifted, turned to him and stared for a moment.

"*Damnation.* I'd about given up on you," the old miner said.

"I almost didn't make it but not because of the Sioux," Fargo said, and quickly told Jethroe everything that had happened. When he finished, Jethroe pushed his hat back on his head and stared at him.

"You know, when you first told me about all of this, I said it was one strange story where nothing seemed to fit. Well, it all fits now, but it's still one hell of a strange story," he commented.

"And nothing that I can figure is going to help me get the boy back," Fargo admitted. "That's what it's all about, and that's what I can't answer. Sheila wants a big posse, enough men just to barge in and save Bobby."

Jethroe made a face. "Hell, a big posse'll never get near enough even to see the boy," he said.

"My thinking too. And a small one might get close enough but wouldn't be strong enough to get the boy," Fargo said. "Got any ideas?"

"Not right off," Jethroe said.

"Maybe luring Bear Chest out to fight while a few men go after the boy," Fargo suggested.

"Maybe." Jethroe nodded. "If Bear Chest will take the bait."

"I'm dog-tired. Think on it, Jethroe, and I'll buy you breakfast in the morning," Fargo said.

"It's a deal. Eggs, biscuits, bacon, and coffee," the old miner said. "Meet you downstairs at the hotel."

Fargo nodded, finished the bourbon and hurried from the saloon as Jethroe returned to staring into his beer. He walked the pinto back to the hotel and felt his body demanding sleep. But as he walked his eyes continually swept the sides of the street, pushing into the dark shadows where the moonlight didn't reach; side alleys, overhands, doorway. But the night stayed quiet, and at the hotel, the desk clerk gave him the same room he'd had before.

Inside the room, Fargo shed clothes, put the latch on the door, and fell across the bed to sleep instantly. But he hadn't slept for more than an hour when he heard the knock. He swung up, the Colt in his hand, as he pulled on trousers. The knock came again, softly insistent, and he slipped the latch open and stepped back. "Come in," he growled, and saw the door push open and Sheila hurry into the room, kicking the door shut behind her.

"What're you doing here?" He frowned. "Trouble?"

She dismissed the question with a shake of her head. "I had to talk to you. I couldn't sleep. I lay awake thinking, and I came up with something," she said. "I had to wait for Sam to fall asleep before I could sneak out."

"Talk," Fargo growled as he sank to the edge of the bed and holstered the gun.

"There's a man who can help us," she said. "An old friend of my first husband. His name's Jack Tumley. I want you to go see him. He once saved a little girl held by the Pawnee back in Kansas. Go see him. Find out how he did it. Maybe he'll have some ideas."

Fargo's lips pursed in thought. "He might. Man does something once, he learns a few tricks. Can't see how it'd hurt any to talk to him," Fargo agreed.

"He lives about half a day's ride. You go straight south out of town till you reach the Salmon. Right across the river you'll see a hill with three houses. Jack Tumley lives in the top one," Sheila said.

"You're coming along, aren't you?" Fargo said.

"No. Sam will be watching me like a hawk. Besides, you're the only one that can tell Jack about the Sioux camp," Sheila said.

"Suppose so," Fargo agreed. "You sure he's still there? When did you see him last?"

Sheila hesitated, frowned in thought. "About a month or two ago, I'd guess," she said.

"All right, I'll see what he has to tell me," Fargo said, and rose to his feet. "Now I need some sleep."

Sheila nodded and flung her arms around him, clinging to him with a sudden desperation. "I'll never forget you for all you've tried to do," she said.

"I'm not finished yet," he told her as she continued to cling to him.

"I just wanted you to know that," Sheila said, her dark eyes full of turbulence. She reached up, crushed her lips against his mouth, and pulled away, running from the room without looking back. Fargo pushed the door closed, slipped the latch back on, and returned to the bed. This time he managed to sleep through till the morning sun slipped into the room.

He washed and dressed and found Jethroe waiting for him downstairs at the door to the breakfast parlor. "Eat fast," Fargo said as they sat down. "We've a half day's riding to do." He told of Sheila's visit as Jethroe demolished everything brought to him with contagious relish.

"It's worth the time," Jethroe said over his last cup of coffee. "I sure didn't come up with anything last night. Truth is, it seemed to me that the only chance might be to keep watch on the Sioux camp and just wait it out for a chance to sneak in and get the boy."

"Thought of that myself," Fargo said as he walked with Jethroe to the horses waiting outside. "But I just don't like it." Jethroe asked for reasons with a glance. "There's no telling how long we'd have to wait. Mostly, though, it leaves everything to Bear Chest. That's no good. He could decide to slit the boy in half at any time."

"He could," Jethroe agreed grimly as Fargo led the way from town. He rode south as Sheila had directed and found she had been generous in estimating half a day's travel as the sun was into the afternoon sky when he reached the Salmon River. He crossed, and saw the hill on the other side, the three houses atop it. The highest one, however, was without half a roof, one side of the house sagging to the ground. He sent the Ovaro up the hill with Jethroe close behind. When he reached the house, he stared at what was plainly a house long unlived in, dust and cobwebs over the doorless doorway. He turned and frowned at Jethroe, who shrugged.

The frown stayed on his brow as he turned the Ovaro and rode halfway down the hill to the nearest house. A man in an undershirt and trousers stepped out of a chicken yard to peer at him. "Came looking for Jack Tumley," Fargo said. "I was told he lived up there."

"He did once," the man said. "He's dead now."

Fargo glanced up at the sagging house. "When did he die?" he asked the man.

" 'Bout five years ago," the man said. "Sorry." He turned and went back into the chicken yard. Fargo found himself staring at Jethroe.

"What the hell's going on here?" he rasped.

6

"I think you've been had, brother," Jethroe said calmly.

"*Goddamn!*" Fargo swore as the frown furrowed deep on his brow. "Why in hell did she tell me she spoke to Jack Tumley a month ago?"

"So you'd go chasing out here," Jethroe said.

"But why? It makes no damn sense," Fargo returned, disbelief still flooding over him. "No damn sense at all." He paused, and the thought suddenly came to him, spearing into his shocked disbelief. "Unless Sam Monroe made her do it," Fargo thought aloud.

"Made her?" Jethroe asked.

"Easy enough by holding Abigail," Fargo said.

"Why would he have her send you out here?" Jethroe pressed.

"To be bushwhacked again," Fargo said.

"Nobody's come at us all the way out here," Jethroe pointed out, and Fargo muttered a curse.

"All right, but Sheila had to have some reason.

She wouldn't do it on her own," Fargo returned. "Monroe's got to be behind it somehow." He fell silent a moment and thought of how Sheila had clung to him and how he'd felt the sudden desperation in her. He'd taken it as a reaction to all that had happened, but now he knew it had been something more. He wheeled the Ovaro around angrily.

"Let's ride. I'm going to find out what this means," he said as he sent the horse into a fast canter, Jethroe following. But he slowed quickly as the night settled in, and he rode with caution as he scanned every rise, every cluster of rocks, every hollow. He kept to the edge of the trees where the deep shadows held away the moonlight, and Jethroe rode single-file behind him.

But the hours went by without incident, and it was past midnight when they neared the Monroe house. Fargo dismounted and motioned to Jethroe. "What are you thinking?" the old miner said as he slid from his horse.

"I'm thinking Sam Monroe might be just sitting and waiting," Fargo muttered.

"You mean he set all this up so's you'd race back and come charging up to the house?" Jethroe frowned.

"And get a blast of shotgun lead square in the belly," Fargo said. "Yes, it's just the kind of thing that fits Monroe: indirect and devious." Fargo nodded to Jethroe and began to move forward on foot, edging his way along a laurel hedge. The house was dark and silent, not a glimmer of light shining from it, and Fargo crept forward to halt where the hedge reached the rear of the house. He dropped to one knee, listened. Peering at the dark structure, he felt the hairs at the back of his neck grow stiff.

"Something's wrong," he murmured.

"It's late. Could be everybody's asleep," Jethroe said.

"No. Something's wrong. I feel it in my bones," Fargo said as he began to move along the side of the house. He dropped into a low crouch beneath the window ledge and halted beneath a partly open window not far from the door. He strained his ears for a sound—the rasp of steady breathing, a snore, a cough, anything. But there was only absolute silence, and he grimaced as he edged toward the front door, the Colt in his hand. He halted again, reached one long leg out, and pushed against the door. It swung open, and he pulled back as he waited for the explosion of gunfire. But there was only silence; total, absolute silence. Something was wrong, he muttered inwardly again. He leapt forward, spun, and dived through the open doorway, the Colt ready to fire.

But there was still only silence. He found a hall lamp and lit it, stepping back as the glow spread out. He saw the living room behind him. Jethroe stepped into the house with an old single-action Colt in one hand as Fargo crossed the living room to the adjoining room, found another lamp, and lit it. He saw a single brass bed, a dresser, and a chair. Abigail's room, her initials on two leather bags hanging from the chair. Another room opened from it, and he stepped inside. Sheila's bedroom, he saw at once, her clothes strewn about and an old envelope with her name on it atop a low dresser.

"In here, Fargo," he heard Jethroe call, and ran out to where the old miner waited in a third room off the hallway. "Monroe's gone too," Jethroe said, and Fargo scanned the room where the man's clothes were scattered at the foot of a four-poster bed. The bed had been slept in, he noted, one side of the sheet trailing onto the floor.

"He's lit out and took Sheila and Abigail with him," Fargo said through tight lips.

"Why? They'd only slow him down if he's running," Jethroe said.

"They're his hole cards. He knows I'll come after him. He'll use them to make a deal," Fargo said.

Jethroe frowned back. "It doesn't fit right," he said. "He could've taken them last night. He didn't need to make Sheila send you on an all-day wild-goose chase. Nobody tried to bushwhack you. Something just doesn't fit."

Fargo's lips drew back in a grimace as the old miner's words whirled inside him. Jethroe was right, he knew. It didn't come together right. "Then why?" he bit out angrily. "Why'd she send me off? What the hell did it mean?"

Jethroe shrugged helplessly, and Fargo leaned back against the wall and stared at the floor. He found his gaze riveted at the spot where the bed sheet trailed onto the floor, almost as though the man had fallen from the bed and pulled the sheet down with him. Fargo blinked as his eyes bored into the spot. He moved quickly across the floor and suddenly dropped to one knee. "Jesus," he said breathlessly.

"What?" Jethroe frowned.

"Look here," Fargo said, and pointed to a set of long scrape marks on the floor near the edge of the bed. "Heel marks where boots were dragged across the floor—boots with somebody in them," he said. "Dammit, we've had it all backward."

"What are you talking about?" Jethroe asked.

"Look there," Fargo said as he pointed to where the scuff marks led across and out of the room. "Monroe didn't take off with Sheila and Abigail. They took off with him." He rose to his feet as Jethroe stared at the marks. He grabbed the pillow on the bed and swore softly as he saw the tiny drops of dried blood. "They sneaked in while he was asleep, bashed him one for good measure, dressed him, and dragged him out," Fargo said, crossing the room in three long strides. He followed the long scrape marks across the hallway and outside.

"They're leading to the stable," Jethroe said, and hurried on to pull the stable door open. Three stalls were empty, an old brown mare standing in the fourth. Fargo saw the trail scrape across the hay strands that covered the floor.

"They tied him, lifted him onto a horse, and took off," Fargo said grimly. He started to turn away when he spied the small square of notepaper stuck into a crack in one of the posts. He pulled it down, flipped it open, and read aloud. " 'Fargo: Maybe you'll find this. I've gone to get my boy back. I'm bringing the Sioux the only thing that will save Bobby, the one thing that he wants—Sam Monroe. I'm exchanging my son for a rotten, lying, murderer. I knew you wouldn't agree to my doing this, but I know I'm doing the right thing. Abigail has come because she knows the way. I'm grateful for all you've done. Sheila.' "

"I'll be a monkey's uncle." Jethroe whistled.

"There's the reason she sent me off chasing a dead man. She knew I'd never let her do this, damn her fool hide," Fargo swore, and threw an angry, bitter glance at Jethroe. "You know how much exchanging Bear Chest will do, don't you?" he flung out, and Jethroe nodded grimly. "God damn her fool notions," Fargo spit out. "Let's ride," he said as he ran from the stable to the Ovaro. He leapt onto the horse and sent the pinto racing into the night. But he slowed quickly, swearing at his foolishness, and Jethroe caught up to him to fasten him with a jaundiced eye.

"Glad you got yourself some sense back," the old miner muttered. "Done-in horses do a man no good."

Fargo nodded and pulled in under a spread of hickory. The horses had been traveling all day and were in no shape to go on. Sheila and Abigail had a full day's start, and he'd have to make that up somehow, he told himself as he laid out his bedroll and stretched his tired body over it.

"Maybe we'll be lucky. Maybe Abigail will lose the way," Jethroe said.

"She's too damn smart for that," Fargo said bitterly, closing his eyes to welcome sleep.

He was in the saddle again when dawn came, Jethroe following as he set a steady pace and fought down the urge to race the horses. He stopped only twice for water, and they were in the foothills when night came, and he pulled up at a place where the box elder formed a low overhang.

"You've been thinking as hard as you've been riding," Jethroe remarked as they settled down to sleep.

"Yes, all merry-go-round thoughts," Fargo said.

"What's that mean?"

"Thoughts like merry-go-round horses. They keep going around and around and end up in the same spot," Fargo said with anger in his voice. "If we don't catch Sheila and Abigail before they reach the Sioux, there'll be damn little chance to save anybody," he said, and Jethroe grunted agreement. Fargo turned on his side and drew sleep around him until the morning sun came. Fargo set a steady pace again, munching on wild fruits as he rode, and they moved out of the foothills into the lower range of the mountains.

"We'll be reaching the Sioux camp come night," Jethroe remarked, and Fargo's lips turned in at what remained unsaid. They hadn't caught up to Sheila and Abigail yet, Fargo swore silently as he quickened the pinto's pace. When darkness swept over the mountains, he was climbing the long, tree-covered slope to the wide ridge. The three tall tama-racks stood out sharply in the moonlight when he reached the ridge, and he rode past them this time, finding the passage beyond, which the Sioux used with their ponies.

He halted halfway down the sides and dis-mounted. Jethroe did the same, and Fargo tethered both horses to a mountain bush before beginning to move down again on foot. He stayed to the edge of the passage as the Sioux camp came into sight behind a line of shadbush. He moved closer, Jethroe at his heels. The Sioux had two big fires going this time and four bucks patroling the perimeter of the camp. Fargo lowered himself to the ground, motioned for Jethroe to follow, and began to edge forward on his rump. He halted when he was close enough to see the camp clearly, and Jethroe came up alongside him as he peered through the moun-tain brush.

Fargo swept the camp with a long, slow glance and found Sheila first, wrists and ankles bound. She sat against a tree stump, and Bobby was tied beside her. He shifted his gaze and spotted Abigail only a few feet away, tied much like Sheila with rawhide thongs. Sam Monroe was close to her, but he was bound to a stake, stripped down to the bottoms of his underwear.

"There they are," he whispered to Jethroe. "Damn their hides," Fargo said bitterly. "They rode in with Monroe in tow, as though they were exchanging beads and blankets."

"And found that the Sioux don't exchange anything unless they have to, and here they were given a whole damn present," Jethroe muttered. Fargo shifted his glance back to Sam Monroe. The Sioux had already given him a taste of what they had planned for him. The man's body was covered with long, deep, bleeding lines that ran from his chest down to his belly. Probably made by bear claws fastened to sticks, Fargo surmised. Only a beginning. He grunted grimly. Only a beginning. His eyes returned to Sheila. She was unmarked, but he saw that Abigail bore a red bruise over one eye. Knowing Abigail, she had probably tried to kick a Sioux in the groin. His eyes swept the rest of the camp again. Knots of braves sat together near the fire, a few squaws wandered about, and he saw the ponies tethered on the far side of the camp. Jethroe's voice whispered at his side.

"No way, Fargo," the old miner said. "No damn way you're going to break them out of there."

Fargo swore silently at the truth in Jethroe's conclusion, but his eyes continued to scan the camp. As he watched, the flap of the largest tepee opened, and Bear Chest stepped out, the slender, small, black-haired form of his daughter beside him. His hand on her shoulder, the Sioux walked to the captives and halted first before Abigail. He spoke to his daughter, and the young girl's black braids swayed as she nodded.

"What'd he say?" Jethroe asked.

"He asked her if she'd like that one as her own slave," Fargo told him, and watched as Bear Chest halted in front of Sam Monroe. He spoke to his daughter again, and Jethroe's voice whispered at once.

"What now?" he asked.

"He's telling her that tomorrow she will see what happens to those who trick and lie to the Sioux," Fargo translated.

The Indian turned away from Sam Monroe and started back to his tepee with his daughter, pausing in front of Sheila and Bobby.

"He's going to sell the boy to the Plains Cree," Fargo said, and watched Bear Chest take the young girl to the tepee.

The old, toothless crone of a squaw came out and took the girl into the tent as Bear Chest returned to sit with some of his braves. Fargo stared down at the tepee and let the thoughts race and tumble across his mind.

"Maybe there is a way," he murmured to Jethroe, and saw the older man's frown. "Let's get out of here," Fargo said, and began to push himself upward with the palms of his hands.

Jethroe carefully did the same until they were almost to where the horses were tethered. Only then did they turn and climb the rest of the way. "What the hell did you mean back there?" Jethroe asked Fargo when they reached the horses. "You gone plumb loco?"

"Maybe," Fargo said. "But there is a way. You

can call it beating Bear Chest at his own game. Or doing what Sheila wanted to do, but doing it right."

"You're not making any damn sense," Jethroe said.

"The young girl," Fargo said.

"Bear Chest's daughter?" Jethroe frowned.

"She's his prize possession. That's pretty damn plain. He'd bargain to get her back alive," Fargo said. "He'd be half crazy with rage, but he'd bargain. I'm going to take her. She's not under guard. I can get her out."

"You can get yourself scalped, that's what!" Jethroe said. "How do you know there isn't a Sioux buck inside that tepee?"

"He has no reason to keep her under guard. Anyway, I'll have to take that chance," Fargo said. "It's the only damn way we have to save the others, *the only way.*"

Jethroe wrinkled his already wrinkled face still further as he turned thoughts inside himself. "It's a hell of a slim chance," he muttered. "But I guess you're right, it's the only one. We're sure never going to break the others out any other way."

Fargo led the way to the top of the ridge and back to the three tall tamaracks. "You wait here with the horses. I'm going down this way. It'll bring me to the rear of the camp," Fargo said. "I'll have to wait for the right moment. That could take time. It might be daybreak before I get back."

"If you get back," Jethroe grumbled. Fargo's tight jaw was silent agreement as he left Jethroe with the horses and began the climb downward. He used the mountain shrub to hold onto, as he had before, and carefully lowered himself down along

144

the steep slope until he neared the rocks at the base. Two of the sentries patroling the perimeter of the camp appeared just as he reached the first of the rocks, and he flattened himself behind a boulder and lay still. He gave them time to move on before pulling himself to his feet again. He darted forward to the next line of rocks, slipped on to those still closer, and halted. But this time he stayed back from the rocks closest to the camp where the heat of the two fires reached out. He settled down behind a tall boulder with a narrow crevice that let him see through to the camp. The guards continued to make their rounds, he saw, but the four had given way to only two as the night grew deeper.

He watched the two fires burn into embers and saw that Sheila and Abigail slept fitfully, the boy nearest his mother. Sam Monroe hung limp on the stake, he noted, head down, and Fargo's eyes moved to the other side of the fires where the ponies were tethered. Bear Chest stepped from his tepee once, surveyed the camp, and went back inside. The knots of braves that clustered around the campsite had stretched out in sleep, looking like giant pinwheels, and the camp grew still and silent. The only movement was from the two patroling braves.

Still, Fargo waited behind the rocks until he was satisfied that the camp was deep in sleep. He watched the two sentries pass and then slipped out from behind the rocks. He moved quickly on silent cat's feet to the edge of the camp, the tepee that held Bear Chest's daughter directly in front of him. He drew the razor-sharp throwing knife from its calf holster. Holding the blade between his teeth, he flattened himself out on his stomach and began to edge himself across the open ground. The few feet to the tepee suddenly seemed to be yards as he inched himself forward, digging his fingers into the grassy soil to pull himself on.

He halted at the back of the tepee and pushed himself to his knees. He had just about four minutes before the two Sioux sentries returned to the spot, he estimated as he took the knife from between his teeth and pushed the point through the thinned, dressed buffalo hide. He made a small hole and began to use both edges of the knife to cut. When he had cut enough to fully insert the blade, he began the long stroke downward, pausing every few moments to listen to sounds from inside the tent. He felt the little drops of perspiration form across his forehead as he continued the long, slow downward cut until he had a slit long enough for him to peer through. He drew the blade back, put his eye to the slit, and peered into the tepee. The blackness of the interior was broken by a small flame that burned inside a hollowed rock filled with bear grease. It cast just enough light to let him see the young girl asleep on her side atop a pallet, her pubescent little breasts protruding with firm gracefulness. She would grow to be a beautiful Indian maiden, and he disliked making her a pawn in a deadly game. But he had no choice, and he brought his gaze past her to where the old crone of a squaw lay asleep near the girl. The ancient one lay on her back, and he heard the gargled half snores that rose from her throat. The old crone slept on the ground, and a whisk of thick horsetail lay on the ground beside her.

Fargo drew his eye back from the slit and continued to draw the knife downward until the slit was long enough for him to step through. He glanced along the edge of the camp and saw the two Sioux sentries turning the far corner to make their way toward him. He stepped through the slit and crouched down inside the tepee, the knife in one hand, the Colt in the other. He heard the two sentries outside and held his breath. They wouldn't see the slit unless they looked directly at the back of the tepee, and they'd no reason to do that. Fargo waited, listened to the two braves pass by, and let his breath out in a long, slow hiss. One sound and it was all over, he knew. and he turned back to the inside of the tepee and moved across it to the girl.

He was almost at her side when the old crone suddenly sat up, her uncombed, stringy hair sticking out wildly from her head. He knew she hadn't heard him but had come awake with a sixth sense. Her inner sense of danger awakened her, and she stared through the dimness, blinked, and found him. He saw her toothless mouth open up to utter a cackling scream as he scooped up the horsetail whisk and jammed the end of it into her open mouth before she could utter a sound. She fell onto her back with the horsetail filling her mouth as her wizened old frame quivered.

Fargo spun as the girl woke, sat up. He brought a short, chopping blow downward, just enough to put her out, and he caught her as she fell. He lifted her up, tossed her over his shoulder, and climbed through the slit, his long legs churning across the few feet of open ground. He reached the rocks and began to climb as fast as he could, using one hand to grab on to mountain brush and yank himself upward. The sky had begun to lighten, he saw as he climbed with the girl over one shoulder. He was more than halfway up the top when he heard the shouts from below, a murmuring swell of sound that rose up the slope after him. The old crone had finally pulled the horsetail whisk out of her mouth and had screamed the alarm. He knew the camp had erupted in a frenzy of surprise and fury.

He reached the top of the slope, and Jethroe spied him and came on a run with the horse. "We have to find a hiding place pretty damn quick," Fargo said as he put the girl across the saddle and swung onto the Ovaro.

"This way," Jethroe said as he wheeled his horse in a half circle. "I did some exploring while I waited. This hillside is full of side passages, ravines, and hollows." He bent his horse down the side of the slope opposite the tamaracks, swerved into a thick cluster of aspen that turned into a rocky, narrow ravine, and reined up where two big blue spruce all but hid a tall rock. Jethroe circled behind the rock, and Fargo saw the cave set well back. "Maybe a mite close, though," Jethroe said.

"No, that's all the better," Fargo answered. "They'll figure whoever took the girl ran fast and far. They won't even look this close." He slid from the saddle, carried the girl with him, and entered the cave. The dank, musty odor assailed his nostrils at once, but the cave was large enough for horses and men, and he put the girl down against one wall. "We stay holed up here till they've finished racing through the mountains and go back to camp. I figure that'll be by nightfall," Fargo said.

"Then what?" Jethroe queried.

"I wait till morning and go pay Bear Chest a visit," Fargo said. "On my terms, nice and calm."

He turned as he heard the girl stir and saw her eyes open. She stared at him for a moment and pushed herself to her feet. She stood straight, proud, her black eyes holding more defiance than fear. "We won't hurt you," Fargo told her in Sioux as Jethroe stepped to her and began to tie her wrists and ankles. He put a kerchief across her mouth.

"Can't have you yelling out, young lady," Jethroe said as he tied the gag in place and set her back against the wall. The black eyes that stared at Fargo over the top of the kerchief continued to hold only defiance.

"Let's get some sleep," Fargo said, and set out his bedroll across the mouth of the cave. He didn't expect the girl to untie herself, but if she did, she'd have to cross him to get out. He slept, woke occasionally at the distant sound of a war whoop, and returned to sleep. When he finally awoke, refreshed, the sun had lowered itself over the high peaks. Fargo moved carefully out of the cave, listened, and caught the distant sounds of racing ponies. He returned inside to where Jethroe had sat up.

"They're still chasing over the mountains," he said, and slid down to the ground. "Good enough. Another full night's sleep will be fine with me."

"No objections there," Jethroe agreed. He brought some strips of beef jerky from his saddlebag, and Fargo pulled the girl's gag down and offered some to her. She shook her head as her eyes continued to bore him with defiance.

"Suit yourself." He shrugged and put the gag back in place. Night came to plunge the cave into blackness, and Fargo returned to his bedroll and welcomed the extra sleep. He woke twice during the night as he heard the girl move; he knew she was trying to break her bonds. He also knew she'd no chance at doing that, and he returned to sleep.

When morning came, he saw that she had rolled halfway across the cave, and he rose, pulled her to her feet, and brought her back to where he'd put her. He took the gag from her, and she licked her lips as she flung anger and defiance at him with her black eyes. "You've a name," he said in Sioux, and heard Jethroe wake and come over to listen.

"It is not for your tongue," she snapped in Sioux. "Bring me water," she demanded.

He went to the pinto and brought his canteen back as Jethroe untied her wrists so she could drink. When she finished, she handed him the canteen with a stiff-armed, imperious gesture. "Food?" Fargo asked, and she shook her head disdainfully.

"My father will kill you," she said almost matter-of-factly.

"I understood that," Jethroe commented.

Fargo met the anger in her black eyes. "Not if he wants you back," he told her.

"He will kill you," she said. "Let me go, and I will have him spare your life."

"Damn, she's one hard-nosed little thing," Jethroe said.

"A chief's daughter. She's learned how to give orders," Fargo said. "Tie her again." He put the kerchief over her mouth as Jethroe tied her wrists behind once more. He saw the dark and confident certainty in the black eyes. He turned to Jethroe as he went to the pinto. "Time to get the show on the road," he said.

"What if it all blows up in your face?" the old miner asked. "There's no predicting a Sioux."

"Wait here till night. Untie her, and then get hell away from here," Fargo told him.

"Good luck, friend," Jethroe murmured as Fargo walked from the cave with the Ovaro. Outside, he swung onto the saddle and paused at the edge of the tall boulder. Listening, he heard only the sounds of the birds. He rode out, climbed the hillside, and swung onto the top of the wide ridge. He walked the Ovaro slowly and had reached the three tamaracks when he spotted the two Sioux at the same instant they saw him.

He saw them shout and race their ponies toward him, and five more Sioux appeared and raced at him. They raised their voices in wild shouts, and another two braves appeared and headed for him. He kept the Ovaro at a steady walk as they raced up to him and halted, and four had lances they jabbed in the air at him as they shouted. Fargo stared straight ahead and ignored their actions and their shouts, and the Indians fell in to flank him on both sides. They continued to jab the lances toward him, but he continued to ignore them.

When he reached the passage that led down to the camp, he took it and saw another two braves come racing up. They joined the others in muttering and frowning among themselves as they rode alongside him. He kept moving down the passage at a slow walk. The Sioux warriors jabbered and shouted among themselves as they watched him move steadily on, and three drew closer, jabbing their lances to within inches of his face. He forced himself not to react, and not even a facial muscle twitched as he continued to stare straight ahead. The all-important thing was to show no fear, and Fargo knew he was putting on a hell of an act as inside himself his stomach churned. He reached the bottom of the passage, and the camp lay before him. More braves ran up on foot as he slowly walked the horse forward. They jostled each other as they ran alongside him, and out of the corner of his eye he glimpsed tomahawks being waved and arrows pulled back on short bows.

But he stared impassively ahead until he came abreast of the tied captives. His eyes went to Shiela and Abigail as they stared up at him.

"Oh, my God," Sheila murmured, her eyes round with desperate hope.

"Fargo," Abigail breathed, more calm control in her voice. "Can you?" she asked, other words unnecessary.

His lake-blue eyes were hard as he peered down at them. "You two get the damnfool award," he bit out through tightened lips. He tore his eyes from them and moved the Ovaro forward. The Sioux chief had come from his tepee to stand in front of him, the Indian's massive chest looking not unlike a copper wall, his broad, flat face drawn tight, his eyes glittering black coals. Fargo could feel the rage pent up inside the man, and suddenly the old crone burst from a tepee nearby. Fargo watched her jump up and down as she screamed and pointed a bony finger at him.

Bear Chest took a step forward. "The spirit of the mad must live inside you, white man," the Sioux said. "Where is my daughter?"

"She is safe," Fargo said.

"You take my daughter, and you come here in my camp. I will cut your heart out and leave it for the vultures," Bear Chest roared.

"Then you will never see her again," Fargo said, using sign language to implement his Sioux.

"I will keep you here and put the fire to you until you tell me where she is," the Indian threatened.

Fargo kept his face expressionless. "She is dead if I do not return when the sun moves to the high mountains," he said, watching as the Indian held his fury in check as his powerful shoulders quivered and his hands clasped and unclasped.

"Speak," Bear Chest thundered.

Fargo gestured to the captives with a sweep of his arm. "I take these back. You have your daughter," he said, and made the sign for a trade.

"No," the Sioux snapped at once, but Fargo remained calm. The Sioux couldn't give in too quickly. That would mean losing face. Fargo's eyes moved over Sheila and Abigail, paused at Bobby, and went to Sam Monroe. Each stared at him with fear and hope, Abigail the most contained of all. He returned his eyes to Bear Chest.

"I take these back," he said, "you have your daughter." He had added nothing and taken nothing away, offered only one trade.

"No," the Sioux chief repeated.

Fargo shrugged. He made the sign for a trade again and sat back in the saddle and waited. It was only a few moments, he realized, yet it seemed hours as the Indian stared through him. Finally the chief stepped forward to stand before his captives. His eyes moved slowly over Bobby and Sheila and halted at Abigail, stayed for a long pause, and then turned to Fargo.

"The boy and the two squaw for my daughter," he said. Fargo glanced at Sam Monroe and saw the fear in the man's heavy face. He made a sweeping gesture with his arm.

"I take all," Fargo said.

Bear Chest stepped closer to Sam Monroe, and his glittering black eyes took on new hate. "This one stays. He is a jackal of trickery. He stays. You take others," the Indian said.

Fargo grimaced inwardly. "All," he insisted again, and the Sioux chief spun, and his broad face held fury.

"To trade him is to betray my warriors and dishonor the dead. He stays. You take others," Bear Chest roared.

"Your daughter's life," Fargo reminded the Indian.

Bear Chest's face grew tight, and Fargo saw the answer in his eyes before it was given words. Tribal honor was unyielding, beyond bargaining. "She is a Sioux daughter. She will sacrifice herself for the honor of Sioux warriors. She will understand," the Indian said. "He stays, or no trade and everyone dies."

Fargo's eyes went to Sheila and saw her staring at him. "Take it, for God's sake, Fargo. To hell with Sam Monroe," she cried out.

Sam Monroe's voice screamed at once. "Don't listen to her. She's a goddamn crazy woman," the man said.

Sheila half turned to Sam Monroe, and Fargo saw the hate in her eyes as she bit out words. "You were happy to write off Bobby. You tried to stop anyone from saving him. You sent others out to be massacred. You didn't give a damn about them. I don't give a damn about you. You're not worth saving," she flung at him.

"You don't know what they'll do to me," Sam Monroe pleaded.

"I don't give a hoot in hell. I'd be tempted to stay and help them," Sheila shot back.

"Goddamn bitch," Monroe screamed at her.

Sheila brought her angry, desperate eyes back to Fargo. "Too many have already paid for his worthless hide. He deserves to be left. He deserves whatever happens to him. Give me one reason why we should all die because of him. One reason, Fargo," she said.

Fargo mouth was a thin line. "I can't," he admitted. "Not a one."

"Bastard! You can't do this," Monroe shouted, his voice breaking. "You can't walk out of here and leave me to them."

Abigail's voice cut in, soft, almost sad, and Fargo met the direct brown eyes that gazed at him. "Get on with it," she said and he nodded. She was the only one who realized that it wasn't a matter of moral decision, not even of justice or vengeance. Whether Sam Monroe deserved his fate was a judgment of someone far better to decide. He had pressed as far as he could. The Sioux cheif wouldn't yield any further. There was really no choice. He raised one fist and struck it onto the palm of his other hand, the sign that the trade was done, accepted, and sealed.

"No. No," Sam Monroe screamed, his voice a hoarse, strangled sound. Fargo turned to the Sioux chief.

"You bring my daughter now," the Indian said, and Fargo's smile was grim.

"I take these now. Then I send your daughter back," he said. Bear Chest's instant explosion of anger was proof enough of what Fargo had suspected.

"No, my daughter first," the Indian roared.

"I take these first," Fargo repeated.

"*No!*" Bear Chest thundered.

Fargo shrugged. He had begun a deadly game and had to play it out to the end. Anything less would turn victory into death and defeat. He pulled the Ovaro into a tight circle and began to move toward Sheila. Bear Chest shouted, and six arrows slammed into the ground in front of him. He reined up, braced himself as hands pulled at him from both sides, and he was yanked from the horse. Rawhide strips bound his arms to his sides instantly, and he was thrown to the ground almost at Abigail's feet.

"You bring daughter first," Bear Chest shouted. Fargo spat on the ground, and the Indian delivered a kick into his ribs and stalked away. Fargo watched him disappear into his tepee and pulled himself into a sitting position almost beside Abigail.

"What's the matter with you? Do it his way. What's the difference?" Abigail hissed.

"The difference is that I do it his way and none of us leave. You don't learn much from experience, do you?" Fargo answered.

"He made a bargain. I thought honor was important to an Indian," Abigail said.

"A Sioux is still a Sioux. To outsmart a white man is no loss of honor. It's a coup," Fargo said. He settled back against the stump beside her and sighed.

"How can you be so damn calm?" Abigail frowned in exasperation.

"Bear Chest wasn't bluffin, about Monroe," Fargo said. "I hope." He leaned back and waited.

He hadn't long to wait as the Sioux stalked from his tent soon after. He scowled, blustered, and threatened, but Fargo refused to agree. The Indian stalked back into his tepee, made another visit a half hour later, and at his third visit, Fargo peered up at the sun that had begun to move across the sky toward the high peaks. The gesture needed no words, and Bear Chest barked orders at two braves. They leapt forward, yanked Fargo to his feet, and untied the rawhide strips.

"I go with two braves," the Sioux Chief said, and Fargo grunted at the real meaning of the demand. He had refused to trust Bear Chest to keep his bargain, and now the Sioux was saying the same thing to him. Fargo nodded agreement. Bear Chest snapped orders, and Fargo watched as Abigail, Sheila, and Bobby were untied. The boy clung to Sheila as they waited until another Sioux brought their horses.

"Mount up," Fargo said as he swung onto his horse. His eyes paused on Sam Monroe as the man stared at him.

"You can't, goddamn you," the man screamed. "You can't leave me here. Don't do this. I didn't do anything."

Fargo turned away, wishing he could feel more than disgust for Sam Monroe. In the end only one thing counted—Justice. It didn't matter much whether it came from a white man's noose or a Sioux arrow. He waited beside Abigail, and a furrow began to cross his brow. Bear Chest had gone off with his braves to get his pony. He was taking his own sweet time about it, Fargo growled silently, and a moment of uneasiness stabbed at him. The furrow stayed on his brow as the moments continued to stretch until finally he saw the Sioux chief appear from the other end of the camp astride a sturdy, short-legged Indian pony. Two braves followed in single file behind him, and the others gathered in a knot to watch.

"What took so damn long?" Fargo growled in English, but the Indian understood the question from his tone of voice.

"There is no hurry now," Bear Chest said, and Fargo grimaced inwardly, as he didn't like the answer any more than he had the wait. He swung in beside Sheila and Abigail and started from the camp, the Sioux chief coming up behind him. Sam Monroe's screams split the air and stayed with him until he was halfway up the passage to the ridge.

"I guess we did it all wrong," Sheila said.

"You sure as hell did. Amateur night," Fargo spit out.

"It's over now, thanks to you," Abigail put in, and the gratefulness in her voice was real.

"Don't bet on it," Fargo growled, and instantly frowned. "I don't trust that Sioux. He's a bad apple to begin with. Sam Monroe isn't enough for him now. He's too caught up in his hating and killing."

"But you outplayed him. You made the best of it. What can he do now?" Abigail frowned.

"I don't know, but I've a sour feeling inside," Fargo said, and his glance took in both women. "Whatever I say, you do and do it fast, you hear me? No waiting, no questions." Sheila and Abigail nodded, and Fargo cast a glance behind him.

Bear Chest rode on his tail, the two braves staying back in Indian file. Fargo reached the wide ridge and quickly cut down across from the three tamaracks. He found the aspen and the ravine behind the trees and drew to a halt where the big spruce hid the mouth of the cave. He stayed in the saddle as he called out. "Jethroe, it's me. Bring her out," he said.

After a moment he saw the old miner poke his head cautiously out of the cave. Jethroe's glance took in Bear Chest, but he saw Sheila, Abigail, and Bobby beside Fargo.

"Comin' out," he said, and came forward with the young girl in front of him. Fargo watched Bear Chest's eyes go over his daughter in one piercing glance.

"Take her," Fargo said, and the Sioux chief beckoned to the girl. Fargo glanced across at the two braves, and he felt the sharp, stabbing pain in the pit of his stomach. There was only one brave. Only one, he repeated to himself. "Son of a bitch," Fargo hissed. The second brave had faded back the minute they'd reached the cave. He'd slipped silently away, probably on foot, to insure silence, and he was running up to the ridge where the others were waiting by now.

Fargo saw Bear Chest's eyes on him as the Indian realized that Fargo had caught on. Fargo's hand flew to the big Colt, and he fired a single shot. The brave beside Bear Chest flew from his pony as though he'd been yanked off by an invisible rope, and Bear Chest threw himself to one side.

The girl had started to run to him, but Fargo spurred the Ovaro forward, leaned down, and scooped her slender form up with one arm and flung her facedown across the saddle.

"Run," he yelled to Jethroe and the others. "Get the hell out of here." He saw Jethroe pull himself onto his horse and start out in a full gallop, Sheila behind him with Bobby, Abigail last, and he saw the fear in her eyes as she cast a glance back at him. "Ride, dammit," he yelled at her, and she disappeared with the others through the trees.

Bear Chest was on his feet, a tomahawk in his hand as he rushed forward. Fargo fired as he whirled the Ovaro around, and the shot only grazed the Sioux. Fargo sent the horse streaking in the other direction from that which Jethroe had taken. The brave that had slipped away had reached the others waiting on the ridge by now. They'd be into the ravine in moments, and Fargo drove the horse up a steep incline, took another mountain slope, and rode diagonally across the terrain and into the high range. But there'd be no outrunning them this time. They were too close, and there were too many of them.

His hand, pressed onto the girl's back, kept her in place as he raced up the rocky, sparsely covered mountains. He could hear the Sioux shouts as they gave chase. Their tough, short-legged ponies were perfect for the mountain country, and Fargo's eyes swept the high land in front of him as he raced on. They'd be in sight of him soon, perhaps within two or three minutes, he realized, and he turned to the right as a steep side of rock rose into the air in a jagged line. A ledge of flat land bordered the crag, and he sent the pinto racing across it. Eyes narrowed, he saw the end of the flat land just ahead of him, and he reined the pinto in as he reached it. He stared down at the straight drop that ended in a toothlike base of rocks. He had expected the flat ledge of land to drop off in a cliff. The game was not ended yet. There were still a few moves left. Damn few, but enough so that if they were played correctly, he might still come out the winner.

He slid from the saddle and pulled the girl with him. He turned, his back to the edge of the cliff, and held her in front of him with one arm around her young, smooth-skinned waist. The horde of racing riders appeared, reined up a few yards from him. Bear Chest leapt to the ground, took a step toward him, the heavy tomahawk in one hand. "You go the wrong way. Now there is only the cliff," the Indian said. "Our arrows will drive you over it."

"I'll have company," Fargo said, and gestured to the girl by tightening his arm around her.

The Indian's eyes narrowed. "A coward hides behind a young girl. Let her go," he said.

"A jackal does not keep his bargain. Bear Chest trades only in lies," Fargo said, and saw the man's massive chest quiver in held-back fury. "Prove you are a chief. Kill me for your daughter," Fargo pressed, aware that the others listened and watched. It was a challenge the Sioux could not turn down. He had turned the final standoff into a matter of honor, and he knew the others would have to accept the results.

"Throw down the gun," Bear Chest said.

"Throw down the tomahawk," Fargo answered.

The Indian threw the tomahawk to the side, the gesture accepting the challenge once and for all. Fargo sent the Colt spinning into a clump of scrub brush to his right and pushed the girl away from him. He quickly moved sideways, away from the edge of the cliff, as Bear Chest began to stalk him. Arms hanging loosely, the man's massive chest and shoulders tilted forward, he moved ahead on his thin legs, looking as though he might topple over.

But he moved with quick, light steps for all his bulk and feinted with one long arm as Fargo ducked away. The Sioux came in again, feinted to the left and then the right—short, quick motions—and charged. Fargo twisted, brought up a sweeping uppercut, but the Indian took it against his huge chest and brought both hands up as one. Fargo only managed to half avoid the blow and felt himself knocked backward.

He tried to plant his feet and had to twist away again as Bear Chest bulled forward, thick arms grasping for him. Fargo ducked, brought a short, hard right into the Sioux's ribs, and the Indian grunted as he stumbled forward. Fargo swung a backhanded blow with his arm which caught the Sioux across the back of the neck and sent him sprawling facedown. He dived for the man, but the Indian rolled, amazingly quick for his upper bulk, and Fargo grabbed only air. He turned and tried to duck away as the Sioux charged again, but his foot slipped, and Bear Chest crashed into him as though he were a battering ram.

Fargo went down, half on his side, turned only a little as the Indian used his weight to pin him down. He got his left arm up in defense as Bear Chest, atop him, started to bring his powerful forearm down onto his windpipe. Fargo's lips pulled back as he tired to hold the Indian off with one arm, but the Sioux had him pinned. Fargo felt the thick forearm pressing closer to his windpipe and knew it would be a matter of seconds before it smashed into his throat. He dug the fingers of his right hand into the loose soil, drew it into his palm. With his partially pinned arm he managed to fling the handful of soil up and into the Sioux's eyes. Bear Chest blinked, drew back for an instant, the pressure broken for a split second, but that was enough for Fargo. He heaved his body, got one knee up and into the Indian's side, and threw his attacker from him. As Bear Chest fell to the side Fargo rolled in the other direction and sprang to his feet. He started to race at the Sioux, but swerved away as Bear Chest regained his feet and waited with long, thick arms outstretched.

The Indian barreled toward him again, and Fargo threw a looping right. But he hadn't had the chance to get his proper footing, and the blow only bounced off Bear Chest's cheek as the Indian ignored it and charged without even pausing. Fargo dropped low, twisted away from the arms that tried to seize him, swung a short, hard blow that landed in the Sioux's midsection. The Indian grunted as his momentum carried him onward, and Fargo saw him stumbling as he almost went down. It was the second time he'd seen the weight of the Sioux's huge chest and upper body send him off-balance on his narrow torso.

Fargo started to circle and cursed as he saw Bear Chest dive forward but not at him. When the Indian whirled again, he had the tomahawk in his hand. Bear Chest came at him quickly, the weapon poised to strike, and Fargo went onto the balls of his feet. He ducked, turned, twisted, moved sideways from left to right and back again as the Sioux filled the air with slicing, smashing, circling blows with the short-handled ax.

Fargo didn't even attempt to get in a punch as he had all he could do to dodge Bear Chest's blows, any one of them capable of ending the battle instantly. But as he dodged and ducked, he watched the Indian's feet and saw that after every raging blow with the tomahawk Bear Chest half stumbled as his upper weight carried him off-balance. By now the Indian was breathing hard, tired by the succession of wild blows that had struck only air. He paused, halted, moved in more slowly, and Fargo fainted with a left, and Bear Chest pulled back. Fargo's right drove in at once, a short, straight blow that caught the Sioux on the point of the chin. Bear Chest went back and down on one knee, but Fargo saw that there was as much surprise as pain in the man's eyes. He held back rushing in. Bear Chest rose to his feet, and rage filled the broad, flat face. He came at the elusive opponent, who refused to let his head be split open, and the Sioux Chief's black eyes darted back and forth as Fargo gave ground.

Bear Chest moved to his left, and Fargo gave ground again. The Indian moved to his right, and again Fargo backed, noting the tiny, tight grimace of satisfaction on the man's mouth. Bear Chest was backing him toward the edge of the cliff, and Fargo kept his face expressionless as he took another step back to avoid a swiping arc made by the tomahawk. The Sioux moved forward quickly now, swiping again, and Fargo backed once more. Bear Chest smelled victory, Fargo knew, casting a quick glance behind him. He was almost at the edge of the cliff when he crouched, letting the Indian come in with another swipe of his weapon.

This time, as he avoided the blow, he let himself seem to stumble. He went down on one knee at the very edge of the cliff. Bear Chest gave a roar of triumph as he charged, tomahawk raised high in one hand, ready to bring it smashing down on his foe. Fargo forced himself to stay frozen in place as he measured split seconds. As the Sioux's massive chest loomed up directly in front of him, he catapulted himself forward in a low dive. He slammed into the Indian's narrow torso just above the knees, and the weight of Bear Chest's upper body did the rest. The Sioux flew headlong across him, unable to control his unbalanced body. Fargo watched the Sioux's legs disappear over the edge of the cliff, the man's wailing scream filling the air.

Fargo rose to one knee and pushed himself fully to his feet. He looked over at the line of Sioux warriors on their horses, their eyes riveted at the edge of the cliff. He walked to the clump of brush and retrieved his Colt and saw the Indian girl standing at the side of the warriors, her face expressionless. Slowly, soundlessly, the Sioux turned their ponies around. One lifted the girl onto his pony, and Fargo watched as they moved across the flat land. It had been a final duel of honor, and they would honor the winner. It was their way. None so much as glanced back as they slowly rode on, disappearing into the trees at the far end of the flat land.

Fargo drew a deep sigh from the depths of his chest, letting the air slowly escape his lips with a soft hissing sound. Everyone else should have put distance on by now, and he'd no desire to chase after them. He was tired, his body aching, and night had started to lower itself. He wanted only a long night's sleep. He'd catch up with the others in time, perhaps not until they reached Ironwood. Maybe that'd be best, he reflected, give everyone a chance to settle themselves. He climbed onto the Ovaro and rode across the flat land and down the first steep slope. Night threw its black blanket across the land while he was still in the high range, and he found a rock hollow and welcomed sleep.

He woke with the morning sun and breakfasted on apples he found along the way. He hadn't made his way far when he reined to a sharp halt as he saw the aspen to his right and slightly below quiver in a long line. He frowned, peered down, and caught the sight of bronzed riders moving fast. Movement to his left caught his eye, and he turned to see another band of Sioux braves riding fast along the line of a ridge. A third band of riders came into sight above and behind where he had halted. Six, he counted, riding spread out down the mountainside. Fargo's frown deepened as he moved back into the trees and watched the two bands below as they moved back and forth across the mountain terrain.

They were searching for something, he muttered silently. Why? The question hung in his mind, no idle thought. Were they on a new rampage of killing, he asked himself. It was too soon, dammit, he answered himself, too quick and too soon. It took time to choose a new chief. There were ceremonies, rituals, and councils to be held, and they wouldn't go off on a killing spree without a new chief. His pondering broke off as he saw the band above him on the mountainside half turn and move toward where he hid. He pushed the pinto through the trees, spied a rocky pathway that led down, and took it past a flat slab of stone until he found a crevice just wide enough to hold a horse and rider. He pushed in as deeply as he could and halted. By standing atop a narrow rock ledge he could peer through a crack and see the land in front of him.

The Sioux came into sight, and he watched as they swept by and fanned out through the trees below. They were seaching, unquestionably scouring the mountains, he told himself again. He could only think of himself as their quarry. But that didn't fit. They'd honored his victory. They'd keep that honor for a lot longer than overnight. They'd hold to it until there was a new chief or until time wiped the slate clean. But there'd been neither time nor a new chief, and yet they rode hard in their search. Fargo grimaced, unable to put it all together, but he knew one thing. It meant staying in heavy tree cover, staying constantly alert, riding carefully, and taking three times as long to make his way. But he had no choice. Maybe they'd leave him alone, and then maybe they wouldn't. He wasn't about to risk finding out, and he waited until the nearest band of riders had gone on far across the mountainside before he backed the Ovaro out of the crevice.

He moved carefully and slowly through the stands of spruce and aspen, pausing often to scan the land for signs of the three Sioux search parties. The hours slid away as he saw the bronzed riders continue to search along the land below him. He rode with extra care and made certain he didn't show himself or move the thick brush enough to attract a sharp-eyed Sioux's attention. When dusk finally came to color the mountains in deep lavender he felt the tiredness of a day of tension-filled riding where every turn was a dangerous choice, every path one more effort to evade the Sioux. When he finally saw the distant movements of the trees that showed the Sioux climbing to return to their camp, he breathed a sigh of relief and bedded down with the night.

He finished the last of the cold beef jerky,

stretched out of his bedroll, and tiredness brought sleep to him almost at once. But like a mountain cat, his wild-creature hearing never fell totally under the spell of sleep, and every little night sound woke him. Sleep became a restless, fitful thing. It was made more so by the day of tension that still clung to him, he knew, and he swore at himself as he embraced the last few hours of slumber before the dawn.

The sound, when it woke him, came with the first dim, gray light of day. His eyes snapped open as he heard the rustle of branches, close to where he lay. He remained motionless as he listened. The sound came again, and his hand reached out to where the big Colt lay at his side. "Don't try it, you son of a bitch," the voice rasped.

Fargo sat up, peered through the dim, gray light into the brush, and wondered if he had had a nightmare, a voice he could only be hearing in his dreams. But the voice came again, unmistakable, impossible to deny. "You're a dead man, you bastard," the voice called out in a harsh half whisper.

"Monroe," Fargo muttered as he stared into the brush. The leaves moved, and Sam Monroe came into sight, a big, old Smith and Wesson Model One in his hand. The bands of chasing, searching Sioux were suddenly explained by the wild-eyed figure in front of him. "How'd you get away?" Fargo growled.

"They all went off and left the few squaws," Monroe said. "I made a noise and held my breath. The squaws thought I'd dropped dead. They cut me down. I killed all of 'em, even found my gun."

"And got away before the braves came back," Fargo finished.

"That's right," the man grunted, and almost smiled. "I followed the tracks up to the ridge and saw them lined up waiting. When they took off, I knew they were goin' after you. I hid, waited, and saw them come back finally without Bear Chest. I put the rest together."

"How'd you find me?" Fargo asked.

"I figured you'd be coming down from the high land and I found a place where I could see the mountainside. I spotted you, cut across, and holed up when it got dark. I stayed holed up when the Sioux came out searching for me."

"And you knew I'd be slowed up too," Fargo said.

"I had you spotted when the Sioux showed up. I figured you'd be circling, staying low. When they took off, I came down and picked up your trail before it got dark," Monroe said. Fargo cursed at himself inwardly. His concentration had been entirely on the Sioux and their unexpected behavior. He'd never looked back, never thought about being tailed, much less by Sam Monroe. Thoughts snapped off as the man stepped forward and raised the pistol. "I'm going to blow your head off, Fargo. And then I'm going back to Ironwood and kill those two stinkin' bitches. Nobody turns Sam Monroe over to the goddamn Sioux alive," the man said. "Move over, to the left, away from that gun belt next to you."

Fargo used the palms of his hands to half lift, half push himself sideways a few inches. "More, goddammit," Monroe yelled. "Don't play games with me." Fargo lifted himself again, saw the line of thick brush nearby. He pushed himself another six inches closer to it.

169

"Enough? I sure as hell can't reach the gun from here," he muttered.

Sam Monroe's lips curled back in a grin of triumph. "No, you sure as hell can't," he drawled as Fargo watched him with narrowed eyes. Sam Monroe wanted to savor every last moment of his pleasure.

"Enjoy it, you bastard," Fargo said, and watched the man's grin widen.

"That's what I'm going to do, enjoy every goddamn minute of it," Sam Monroe said. But Fargo's eyes were on the Smith and Wesson. Monroe's finger had drawn back from the trigger a fraction as he continued to let himself enjoy his triumph. A fraction, hardly enough, yet it had to be enough. The thick underbrush was almost at his shoulder, and Fargo pressed palms hard into the ground, twisted as he flung himself sideways.

"Goddamn," he heard Monroe bark as the shot rang out. It grazed his ear as he hit the thick underbrush. He rolled and kept on rolling as Sam Monroe emptied the pistol into the brush, shouting curses with each shot. Fargo felt the bullets slam into the ground just behind him as he rolled. He came up against the trunk of a spruce as the firing ceased.

Sam Monroe was reloading, he knew, and he drew the thin, double-edged throwing knife from its calf holster as he rose to a crouch. "You're a dead man, you bastard," he heard Sam Monroe shout, and he saw the man start into the brush, the reloaded pistol in his hand. Fargo drew his arm back, and aimed, letting Sam Monroe take another half dozen cautious steps forward. The man had the gun raised to fire as his eyes darted from side to side. Fargo dropped to his haunches, picked up a loose pebble, and tossed it to his left. The stone struck a tree noisily, and Monroe spun, firing a furious volley. Fargo's arm flew forward, all the strength of his shoulder muscles behind it. Sam Monroe was still firing into the brush where he'd heard the sound when the thin blade hurtled through the base of his neck from the right side. It stopped only when the hilt smashed into flesh, the point jutting out of the other side of his neck.

Fargo watched the pistol slowly drop from Sam Monroe's fingers as the man staggered, lifted his hands to his throat, and clawed at the object there. A futile gesture. He sank to his knees with one hand still curled around the hilt of the knife, fell forward and lay prone, quivered and twitched, and was still. Fargo stepped forward, went past Sam Monroe's lifeless form, and scooped up his gun belt. The Sioux would be racing down the mountainside again, searching with the fury of those cheated out of revenge. Only one thing would stop their angry search, he knew as he stepped back into the brush with his lariat in hand. He retrieved the throwing knife, wiped it clean on the grass, and put it back in its holster around his calf.

He straightened, peered around in the new sun, and found the tallest tree he could spot at the side of the slope. Wrapping a length of the lariat around Sam Monroe, he dragged the man's figure to the tree, tossed the other end of the rope over a branch, and pulled the lifeless form upward. When he secured the end of the rope to the tree, Sam Monroe swayed from the end of the branch in the morning wind.

"You were right, you rotten bastard," Fargo

muttered. "Nobody turns Sam Monroe over to the Sioux alive."

Fargo walked away, swung onto the pinto, and began the climb down the mountain slope. The Sioux would see the swaying figure soon enough. They would understand, and their furious search would end. They'd be happier to have caught him themselves, but they'd accept the finish of it and turn back. Hell, he couldn't satisfy everybody, Fargo muttered as he rode away.

He rode down through the easiest passages now, with no need to play hide-and-seek with Sioux arrows. He made good time, reaching the foothills with plenty of daylight left. Dusk was just giving way to night when he reached the Monroe house. Sheila came running out as he rode to a halt, her arms around him almost before he was out of the saddle. Her deep, pillowlike breasts pressed against him, and he felt the warm, round belly push into his groin. "Oh, God, I was sure you'd make it," she whispered. "I was sure."

"I'm glad, because I sure as hell wasn't," he said. "Everybody safe?"

"Yes," Sheila said. "Doc Evert in town said it'd take a while for Bobby to come around. He's still in a kind of shock. I'm to stay close to him for now."

"You do that, then," Fargo said. "Jethroe and Abigail?"

"Jethroe's in town. Abigail's at the store. She's closing up about now. She'll be here soon. Come inside," Sheila said, and led him into the house by the hand. "How about a hot bath? I was just getting the tub ready."

"Now, that sounds real inviting," Fargo said.

"This way," Sheila said, and led him behind a

curtain to a tin bathtub. He undressed and sighed happily as he slid into the water. Sheila brought another bucket, poured it in, and came to her knees beside the tub, her hands rubbing across his shoulders. "You know there's nothing I can say, no words that'll mean enough," she said.

"Don't need words," Fargo said.

"Will you stay, Fargo?" she asked.

"No, I can't, honey. Too many trails to follow yet," he said.

Sheila's half smile was rueful. "I expected you'd say something like that," she said. "Remember when you were given orders not to take advantage of me?" He nodded at her smile. "Well, the orders were given to me this time."

"Abigail, of course," Fargo said.

"She let me know I'd no need to do more than be grateful to you. She as much as told me that she'd been taking care of you," Sheila said.

"What'd you say?" Fargo queried as he soaped himself.

"You know Abigail. She's hard to argue with, and I don't want to hurt her. She's been my right hand in all of this," Sheila answered.

"Good enough," Fargo agreed.

"No, not good enough," Sheila snapped. "I've thought of nothing but waiting to be with you, to do my own thanking in my own way. I'm sleeping in the other part of the house with Bobby, on Doc Evert's suggestion. He said Bobby needed to stay just with me for a while." She paused and saw the waiting in Fargo's glance. "He doesn't sleep till real late, but when he does, he's out to the world. Come to me then, Fargo, please."

"Never turn down a lady's invitation," he said as

Sheila rose and left him to finish his bath. He had dried off and started to dress when he heard Abigail rush into the house. She flew into his arms as he stepped from behind the curtain.

"I saw the Ovaro outside," she said, her head buried into his chest. "God, you're finally here. I was afraid something had gone wrong when you didn't come back."

"A hell of a lot went wrong. It just didn't stay wrong," Fargo said.

"Tell me later, when we're alone," she murmured.

"When's that going to be?" he asked mildly.

"Later. Sheila's staying with Bobby in the other part of the house. I'll wait for you in my room," Abigail said, drawing his head down to her. She pressed her lips against his, the kiss warm and hungering, her tongue slipping out to touch his mouth.

"I'll be back," he said, and she stepped away as he drew on his shirt. "There's no need to think about Sheila," Abigail said with sudden primness. "She'll understand. I saw to that."

"If you say so," Fargo agreed amiably, and nodded again to her as he walked from the house. He took the Ovaro and rode into town. Jethroe was where he'd expected to find him, at Dolly's place. The old miner embraced him with a heartfelt hug.

"You sure give a man cat fits, Fargo," Jethroe said.

"It was close, too close," Fargo said, and told him everything that had happened.

"Damn if it wasn't," Jethroe echoed when he finished. "But I can go back into the mountains with half a chance again. Tomorrow I'll go look for that old mule. She's up there with all my gear someplace. I'll find her."

"Good luck, old-timer. You helped a hell of a lot," Fargo said. He left Jethroe with a final, heartfelt handshake and slowly returned to the Monroe house. A dim light came from Abigail's room. He slipped noiselessly inside and knocked softly at the door. She opened to stand before him in a silk nightgown that barely concealed her figure. She pushed the door closed after him and let the nightgown fall from her shoulders to stand beautifully naked before him, her narrow, long-waisted body and the modest, upturned breasts beautifully exciting. Her slightly thin legs planted apart, her narrow hips thrust forward, she seemed to quiver in anticipation.

He reached out, cupped his hand around one upturned breast, and his thumb pressed into the soft, pink nipple. "Ah, ah," Abigail breathed, and he shed his clothes quickly as he felt himself responding to her slender beauty. As he shed the last piece of clothing Abigail all but leapt on him, her arms clasping around his neck, the thin legs drawing up to wrap around his waist and dig into the back of his legs. His organ pushed through the dark triangle and flattened against her lean belly. He fell onto the bed with her clasped around him, and she began to move her pelvis back and forth, the wild thrusting almost instant. He drew from her, stretched upward, and her legs fell away.

"Slow, this time, honey. Slow," he told her, and pressed his fingers hard against the already moist, dark portal.

"Oh, God . . . oh," Abigail cried out, and tried to pull back wildly. But he held her down and in place.

His mouth found the modest breasts, pulled gently and caressed, and he let his fingers slowly draw over the liquid lips. Her cry was a soft moan of delight. He moved slowly, gently. He stroked, caressed, touched, and her lean body writhed as she cried out with little moaning sounds. Each time she would begin to gather her wild, frenzied wanting he held her down, continued to soothe her as he stroked. "Yes, yes . . . oh, so good, good, oh, Fargo," Abigail gasped as he slowly began to quicken his movements, letting her gather herself into savoring her ecstasy.

He thought he had done the task, brought her to slow, sweet pleasure when he moved over her, letting his throbbing maleness find its way into the soft darkness.

With a sharp cry that burst from her like a shot, Abigail drew back and hurtled herself forward, slamming her pubic mound hard against him, pushing all of her over his pulsating shaft. Her legs came up, clasped around him, fell away, and she drew back and slammed forward as she had done each time before. Her almost brutal wanting was beyond resisting, and he drew back and thrust in with her as she hurled herself into him.

"Ah, ah, ah," Abigail coughed out with each hurtling thrust, until suddenly he felt her fingers dig into his back, the furious thrusting motions halting as she quivered, and she rose up on her heels, arched back with him still inside her. She screamed as she came, her entire body made of tiny, thrusting motions. As quickly as a flame snuffed out, she fell back and lay limply beneath him. Only a soft, moaning sound of utter satisfaction gave proof that she hadn't passed out.

He finally drew from her and lay beside her, and she curled up against him, her eyes instantly closing in sleep. He took in her narrow figure, the thin legs half drawn up, and she seemed so very young. But she opened her eyes suddenly, stared at him, and pushed herself onto one elbow. "Stay here with me, Fargo," she said. "I'm going to help Sheila run the store. You could run it with us."

"Sorry," he told her. "Come morning I'm heading out."

"You could stay a while longer," she protested.

"Yes, but that'd only make it harder to leave. For both of us," he said.

"Will you come back?" she asked, the direct brown eyes wide.

"I might. You never know where tomorrow takes you," he said.

She reached out, took his hand and pressed it into the dark portal. "Come back, Fargo. Come back and make love to me again. I'll wait for you," Abigail whispered. She pushed downward with her torso, and he let his fingers slip across the moist, dark flesh as Abigail gave a tiny moan. He stroked, ever so gently. Her moans became tiny whimpers of pleasure, and finally he heard the deep, even sound of her breathing as she fell into the deep sleep of total satisfaction.

He lay beside her as she curled against him and saw the moonlight begin to lengthen across the windowsill. He moved slowly, carefully, from beside her and gazed down at her. She never stirred as she lay on her side, knees partly drawn up. He slipped on trousers and carefully turned the doorknob so the latch wouldn't click. He made his way through the dark hallway to the other part of the long house and saw a closed door at the far end of a hallway where the moon through the window afforded the only light. The door opened as he reached it, and he saw Sheila in a robe and, behind her in a small bed, the young boy's sleeping figure. She drew him into the room, led him across the floor, and into an adjoining room where a lone bed occupied the center of the floor. "He won't wake now," Sheila said as she closed the door. "And I can't wait."

She came to him, her hands unbuckling his belt, sliding his trousers to the floor as she wriggled from the robe. The pillowy breasts came against him at once as she pulled him with her onto the bed, and he buried his head into their deep softness. He felt her fingers groping for him, finding him, stroking at once, and her full-fleshed thighs pressed into his legs. He came on top of her soft, fleshy figure and drew one big breast into his mouth and then another as Sheila rubbed her convex little belly sideways against him. Her moans were tiny guttural sounds, low rumblings of pleasure as he caressed the big, pink-brown nipples with his lips, his mouth pulling on each and circling each with a dance of sensual delight.

"Fargo, Fargo . . . make it so I'll never forget, so it'll last me forever," she pleaded.

"Forever's too long a time, honey," he said. "But I'll make it last long enough." He rolled with her, his organ once again a full, spearing, warm shaft of pleasure, and he entered her. He heard her low, rumbling cry of ecstasy. He rode with her, each stroke slow and long, and Sheila's moans were low, groaning cries. Her large, pillowy breasts lifted high, quivered, fell back, and lifted again as she arched her full hips under him.

"Oh, oh, yes . . . aaaah." Sheila groaned and moaned, and the sounds seemed to come from some hidden recess deep inside her. He stayed with her, slowed when she tried to hurry, brought her over and over to the rim of ecstasy and held her there until finally, her arms clasped around his neck, she pulled his face roughly into the twin, soft mounds. He felt the full little belly come up to slap against his muscled abdomen.

"Now, now. It's now," Sheila said from deep inside her throat, and her full-fleshed thighs folded themselves around his hips, her torso lifting, heaving, shaking. Her screams were gasped groans as she exploded with him, a tremendous, heaving deep cry spiraling out of her as she held in that eternal moment when the world was made only of ecstasy.

When she collapsed beneath him, her hands came up to cup his face, and he saw the slow smile on her lips. She folded herself half atop him and was asleep in moments. It had seemed quick, but he knew it had been slow, filled with delayed pleasures, and the night had moved closer to another dawn. He let himself sleep beside Sheila until the morning came, sunlight creeping into the room. She made only a tiny sound as he lifted her soft breasts from his chest and rose from the bed. He watched her turn on her side, knees drawn up, the sound of deep and steady breathing escaping her lips. Sheila was hard asleep again as he pulled trousers on and started from the room. He tiptoed across the adjoining room where the boy turned in his bed but remained asleep.

He hurried down the length of the house and back

into Abigail's room where he slipped noiselessly inside. He shed his trousers and gently lowered himself onto the bed beside her. Abigail stirred, made a tiny murmured sound, but her eyes stayed tightly closed. He let himself have another hour of sound sleep beside her. As the sun streamed into the room he woke, rose, used the big basin of water to wash, and finally pulled on clothes. Abigail turned once but remained asleep. When he finished dressing, he leaned down and woke her. It took a few moments, but she finally snapped her eyes open, stared at him, and brought the morning into focus.

She swung from the bed and took in his fully dressed form. "Didn't want to leave without saying good-bye," he said, and she pulled on a blouse and skirt with a half pout on her face. "Maybe I should have," Fargo remarked.

"No," she said quickly. "I'm glad you woke me." She walked from the house with him, clung to him a moment longer beside the pinto. "Come back soon. Try," she said.

"Maybe," he allowed, and pulled himself onto the horse.

Abigail looked to the far end of the long, low house. "I'm surprised Sheila's not here to say good-bye. She's usually up by now." She frowned. "I'll get her."

Fargo turned the pinto around. "No, don't bother her," he said. "She's sleeping late this morning." He prodded the pinto forward, and the horse had gone perhaps a half dozen yards when Abigail's voice cut through the morning.

"Fargo, you bastard," she screamed. "I hate you. I'll never have anything to do with you if you do come back here. Never, do you hear me? *Never!*"

He paused and glanced back at her with a smile. "I hear you," he said, "but I don't believe you."

He sent the horse into a canter as her hiss of exasperation and anger followed him. He headed out into the wild places where words were only echoes and each trail a new tomorrow.

1861—Utah Territory. A grim land of alkali flats and vaulting canyons where outlaws and vultures come to feed—and to die.

This time Fargo was almost certain.

The shorter one was a little too squat, maybe. But the other one, the tall son of a bitch, he sure as hell had that look about him Fargo remembered—a wild, crazy look, so that even when he went to reach for his coffee, there was menace in his movement. He moved about the campfire with quick, stalking moves, his piercing glance constantly sweeping the surrounding timber. He appeared to be a man forever restless, like an engine that could never be throttled down. Watching him tending to the horses a moment before, Fargo had noted his quick, rough movements and the casual, unfeeling cruelty with which he handled the horses, especially when he led them off to graze near the stream below the camp.

From a pine-stippled ledge about twenty feet above them, Fargo watched as they wolfed down their supper. They were sitting on two logs they had dragged up to the fire and were bent hungrily over their tin plates, shoveling the beans and bacon into their gaunt faces. Fargo had been following both of them from Cedar City, more certain with each mile he covered that now, at long last, he had overtaken the two men he had been seeking all these years. They were the right age, and they had the same pedigree as those who had shot down his parents.

A mile out of Cedar City the two men had raided a settler's cabin, shot the settler down in cold blood, then set fire to his cabin and ridden off with their booty. Had Fargo not been tailing them, there would have been no witness to their crime. As it was, he was furious with himself for not having been close and fast enough to stop them. Though it would have been one gun against two, it was a match Fargo would not have avoided.

But now they were within reach.

He pushed himself back off the ledge and stood up, a man so tall that his head brushed lightly the branches of the pine tree under which he stood, branches that began more than six feet from the ground. He had been in a cramped position for some time and took this opportunity to stretch his massive, buckskin-clad shoulders. Then he took off his hat and combed back his unruly black hair with long, talonlike fingers, not once taking his lake-blue eyes off the two men below him, gazing down at them like some fierce eagle ready to drop like a thunderbolt from the sky.

His six-gun heavy in his hand, he backed off the ledge and slipped silently down through the pines until he was less than twenty yards from the two men. It was close to dusk, and the light from the campfire bathed the two men's unshaven faces in a livid, dancing light. As Fargo stepped out of the pines, his six-gun leveled on them, the two men caught the movement out of the corner of their eyes and turned swiftly to face him. The taller one jumped up. His smaller, bowlegged companion remained seated on the log.

"Don't go for your guns," Fargo told them.

Immediately both men raised their hands. "Put down that gun, mister," the shorter one said. "You don't need that—if it's coffee and grub you want. We got plenty of both."

"That ain't what I want."

"We don't know you, stranger," the tall one said, his voice a low snarl. "You got no call to draw down on us." The man was edging back to get the fire between him and Fargo.

Fargo took a few quick steps closer, leveling his gun on the man's chest. "Stand right where you are, mister," he said. "Take one more step back and I'll ventilate you."

"Hey, now! What you got agin' us?" the smaller one protested. "We ain't never done you no harm."

The tall one's eyes narrowed. "Hey, now. You any kin to that settler we ran into back there?"

"You mean, the one you killed?"

The tall one shrugged. "Listen, mister, that wern't no fault of our'n. That crazy son of a bitch went for his iron."

Fargo did not care to argue the point. "I'm no kin to the settler," he said. "Now just stand easy."

"Damn it, man!" the fellow snarled. "What's your quarrel with us?"

"It goes back a ways," Fargo said, taking a step closer. "Now unstrap your gun belts, both of you."

As both men dropped their hands to their gun belts, the smaller one reached into the fire and flung a blazing piece of firewood at Fargo. As it whipped through the air toward him Fargo ducked quickly to one side and fired. The .45 slug plowed into the small fellow's side, slamming him off the log and into the blazing fire.

At the same time his companion fired at Fargo, sending a bullet into his right thigh. As the slug punched into his thigh Fargo's leg went flying out from under him, and he struck the ground face-down, hard. He had sense enough to lay where he fell, his cocked six-gun still clutched in his right fist.

He could hear the small one squealing like a stuck pig as he floundered feebly in the campfire's flames and then the sound of the taller one pulling his companion out of the fire. There was a short, curt conversation between the two, after which the taller one left his companion and advanced on Fargo. Fitting his boot under Fargo's waist, he flung the Trailsman over onto his back.

As Fargo's head flopped over he looked out from under his nearly shut eyelids and saw the tall man staring down at him, his lean, wolfish face cold with resolve. In the light from the still-blazing campfire Fargo caught sight for the first time of a livid scar running across the man's throat. Fargo had seen such scars before. It was a rope burn, the kind made from a hangman's rope.

The tall fellow kicked Fargo viciously in the side. Satisfied that Fargo was unconscious, he sent a dart of chewing tobacco at Fargo. As it splattered on the ground beside Fargo's head the man straightened up and cocked his revolver. Doing his best to block out the surging pain in his thigh, Fargo rolled over quickly, came up on one knee, and flung up his cocked revolver. It jumped in his hand as he fired, the slug catching the tall man's gun hand. The man's gun went flying in an expolsion of raw flesh and severed fingers. Thumb-cocking swiftly, Fargo fired again, this second slug catching the man in the left shoulder, sending him staggering back. With a scream of pain and outrage he caught himself, then turned and ran.

Fargo pushed himself erect and brought up his Colt, but he could get off only one more shot before his thigh wound caused him to drop back down onto the blood-slicked grass, his head spinning sickeningly. He heard dimly the quick pounding of hoofs as the man rode off. As the sound faded into the night Fargo holstered his Colt and dragged himself over to the one who had fallen into the fire.

The wounded man was in a fearful condition. The lower portion of his face had lain in the flames and was now cooked raw, the skin peeling off one side of his face. A quick examination of the man's chest wound told Fargo that it was fatal. The bullet had caught the man squarely in the chest, then ranged up into the left lung. He was breathing painfully now, in sort, shallow gasps.

As Fargo looked down at the dying man his eyes flickered open. "Who . . . who in blazes *are* you?" the man gasped. "Was it Martha sent you?"

"Martha?"

"My wife."

"Hell, no. It wasn't your wife sent me. Where you two from?"

"Nebraska."

Fargo frowned. "How long you been out here?"

"We just got here last week. Took the stage to Provo."

"That the truth?"

"Shit, mister! What's the sense of my lyin' to you now? I'm a gonner."

"How come you two came West?"

The man coughed painfully and looked up in weary despair at Fargo. "What the hell is it to you? Why you got to know?"

"Just tell me!"

The man laughed, then began to cough. "Hell, we just got sick of our wives—and our jobs. That's all. We thought . . ." He began coughing again, and when he continued, his voice was considerably weaker. ". . . thought we'd try the gold fields . . ,"

In that instant Fargo realized that this man before him and his companion with the rope burn could not be the two for whom he was searching. Yet even so, it was difficult to believe that these human scorpions could be only recent recruits to the owl-hoot trail. The manner in which they had scourged that settler back there revealed a cold-blooded ruthlessness that indicated many years of apprenticeship.

"You two kept your noses clean in Nebraska, did you?"

The fellow smiled feebly. "Hell, no! Clawson and me, we been raisin' our share of hell for a long time now. And you wait, mister. Clawson's a real mean son of a bitch. He'll get you for this."

"That thought give you some comfort, does it?"

For a long moment the little man looked up at Fargo, as if he were debating whether or not to reply. Then he smiled and closed his eyes. A moment later his face settled as he gave up the ghost.

Fargo pushed himself away from the dead man and examined his own thigh wound. The blood was coming from it in a steady, dark stream. Already he was feeling dangerously light-headed. He slipped out of his buckskin shirt, folded it around his wound, then tightened his belt around it to stem the flow of blood. The last thing he remembered was tugging on the belt.

Then darkness smote him like a fist.

Exciting Westerns by Jon Sharpe

*Prices slightly higher in Canada

**Buy them at your local
bookstore or use coupon
on next page for ordering.**

Exciting Westerns by Jon Sharpe

(0451

☐	THE TRAILSMAN #37: VALLEY OF DEATH	(133374—$2.75
☐	THE TRAILSMAN #38: THE LOST PATROL	(134117—$2.75
☐	THE TRAILSMAN #39: TOMAHAWK REVENGE	(134842—$2.75'
☐	THE TRAILSMAN #40: THE GRIZZLY MAN	(135261—$2.75)
☐	THE TRAILSMAN #41: THE RANGE KILLERS	(135725—$2.75)
☐	THE TRAILSMAN #42: THE RENEGADE COMMAND	(136225—$2.75)
☐	THE TRAILSMAN #43: MESQUITE MANHUNT	(136640—$2.75)
☐	THE TRAILSMAN #44: SCORPION TRAIL	(137744—$2.75)
☐	THE TRAILSMAN #45: KILLER CARAVAN	(138112—$2.75)
☐	THE TRAILSMAN #46: HELL TOWN	(138627—$2.75)
☐	THE TRAILSMAN #47: SIX-GUN SALVATION	(139194—$2.75)
☐	THE TRAILSMAN #48: THE WHITE HELL TRAIL	(140125—$2.75)
☐	THE TRAILSMAN #49: THE SWAMP SLAYERS	(140516—$2.75)

Prices slightly higher in Canada

THE OLD WILD WEST

There's an epidemic with 27 million victims. And no visible symptoms.

It's an epidemic of people who can't read.

Believe it or not, 27 million Americans are functionally illiterate, about one adult in five.

The solution to this problem is you... when you join the fight against illiteracy. So call the Coalition for Literacy at toll-free **1-800-228-8813** and volunteer.

Volunteer Against Illiteracy. The only degree you need is a degree of caring.